The Scottish Duke

Of Valor and Honor, Book 1

By
Jessica A. Clements

ARE YOU SIGNED UP FOR DRAGONBLADE'S BLOG?

You'll get the latest news and information on exclusive giveaways, exclusive excerpts, coming releases, sales, free books, cover reveals and more.

Check out our complete list of authors, too!

No spam, no junk. That's a promise!

Sign Up Here

www.dragonbladepublishing.com

Dearest Reader;

Thank you for your support of a small press. At Dragonblade Publishing, we strive to bring you the highest quality Historical Romance from some of the best authors in the business. Without your support, there is no 'us', so we sincerely hope you adore these stories and find some new favorite authors along the way.

Happy Reading!

CEO, Dragonblade Publishing

Prologue

Edinburgh, Scotland

"YOUR GRACE!" CAME a shout from the door of his bachelor's quarters in Edinburgh. Ioan glanced around him and noticed the bulges under the sheet of his bed. He chuckled to himself and momentarily forgot about the urgent voice from behind the door.

It hadn't alerted him in the slightest that the person on the other side had called him "Your Grace."

His father was the duke. His father was "Your Grace." Why was the idiot waking him at this godforsaken hour?

"*Your Grace!*" the person shouted again.

Ioan tried to get out of his bed without waking the other occupants—and failed.

Damn, whatever the blasted fool wants better be important, he thought as he padded across the wood floor to the door.

He opened the door, but he did not expect to see a footman from Rathdrum Hall. The look of sheer grief on the man's face struck him first. "What's wrong?"

"Your father and brothers are dead, Your Grace. You are needed at the Hall posthaste," the footman replied.

Dead? All of them—dead? That couldn't be. Too stunned to even let it show on his face, all Ioan could do was shake his head. Surely, this was some joke. "Are you sure they are dead?"

"Yes, Your Grace." The footman shifted back and forth on his feet.

Ioan nodded. "I need some time to get into my riding attire, and then we will be on our way."

Chapter One

Rathdrum Hall, Scotland
Three months later

IOAN DRUMMOND, THE thirteenth Duke of Rathdrum, was beside himself. In school, he had excelled in mathematics and the sciences, but when it came to household accounts—well, he felt overwhelmed by the immensity of the estate's ledgers.

He was never meant to take over the dukedom. That honor would have been placed on his eldest brother, Noah, who had been trained in the stewardship of the accounts. Ioan, on the other hand, was meant for the army, a gentleman soldier with a commission bought and paid for by his father. He wanted to have the choice to fight for his country—and a great honor it would have been!—but that honor had been bestowed on a distant cousin of his from Shropshire.

Ioan sat at his desk, drumming his fingers against the wood, letting his mind drift back to the day that his whole world changed *Damn and blast it all!* He had to stop letting his mind go back to that moment. He didn't want to work on the accounts. He wanted to find whoever had killed his family. He shifted in his chair—he needed to replace the padding—and realized he needed a break. No, what he really needed was a man of affairs to take on these duties Then he could do what he wanted—no—needed to do.

He turned to the wall and eyed the bellpull. As he was reaching for it, he heard the doorknob to his study jiggle. How did his butler know he was going to call for him?

"Your Grace?" Jeffers, the Rathdrum Hall butler, called from the doorway.

"Do we have the confirmed cause of death for my father and brothers? I don't remember if I asked for it—"

"We do, Your Grace, and you never asked to view it. Would you like me to retrieve it from my rooms?" Jeffers eyed him keenly.

Ioan glanced up at the man. His salt-and-pepper hair was trimmed short, his eyes a startling aquamarine, and his stately presence reminded Ioan of—no, it couldn't be. He would have to ask about the man's resemblance to his father later.

"Have you read it?" Ioan pushed the chair back and stood up, hands clasped behind his back.

"I have, Your Grace. As the doctor stated, there was no foul play, and it couldn't have been murder." Jeffers shuffled his feet.

"Yet, it seems you have a different theory?"

"Yes, Your Grace. Your father had just hired a new footman, Bryson MacKenzie. Don't ask me why your father would ever hire a MacKenzie, but he did. Something was off about the lad, Your Grace. Three days later, your father and brothers were dead."

"Are you suggesting that this MacKenzie was hired to murder my family?" Ioan rose and paced back and forth behind his desk.

"I have no evidence of the truth, Your Grace—"

"Jeffers, stop calling me 'Your Grace.'"

Jeffers glanced at him with a brief smirk on his face before going back to his normal grimace.

"Of course, sir. I think that you should speak with your father's friend at Whitehall. Whatever happened to your father and brothers may be related to whatever they were working on."

Ioan felt a shock. He couldn't imagine any one of the three men who worked for Whitehall acting as spies. Of course, that may have been the point. Parties, balls, fetes, and routes were the best ways to get information. His family was always invited to the best the Season had to offer.

"I will plan to attend the London Season and maybe speak with our friend at Whitehall. Perhaps, as you said, he has a clue of what they were working on—or, at least, something that can point me in the right direction."

Ioan waved Jeffers away with a brief "thank you" and then put pen to foolscap to plan a meeting with Lord Tarleton.

IF THERE WAS anything that Ioan hated more than traveling great distances, it was the London Season. He hated that he would have to be around the simpering misses, the doddering old dragons, and the infernally persistent mamas of the *Ton*. He liked his privacy and his quiet and peaceful life in the Highlands of Scotland. He couldn't seem to tolerate the noise and stench of town living since his father and brothers were murdered.

That wasn't to say that his mother, God bless her, hadn't taught him the finer points of being a gentleman in the upper echelons of English society. He knew the dances; he knew the etiquette; he knew how to dress the part of a well-appointed gentleman; and he knew how to navigate the murky waters of the *Ton*.

That thought had Ioan laughing. Out of all of his brothers, he was the most cavalier with his choices in mistresses, and he tended to attract women of ill repute. He was sure his brothers had all had mistresses as most men of society did. Ioan, though, flaunted his conquests and enjoyed casting them in his father's face. Thinking back, Ioan knew he shouldn't have done quite such a thorough job of it.

"Your Grace, you have a visitor." As he sat in his offices, Jeffers's voice pulled him out of his thoughts.

A visitor? Who would be visiting him here at the Hall? No one came to Scotland to visit. Even his best friends refused to make the journey, not that he blamed them.

Ioan sighed. "Who has called?"

"Master James, Your Grace."

Even though his friend James had recently inherited a title, his ever-faithful butler couldn't stop calling the man by his old moniker.

"I will speak—" Ioan stopped mid-sentence as his childhood friend strode past Jeffers and into his study.

"Thank you, Jeffers, but you took a bit longer than I was willing to wait, sitting on those dainty chairs in the morning room—where you left me." James winked at the butler.

Ioan was secretly glad that his lighthearted friend had traveled so far out of his way to visit. He waved Jeffers off and turned his attention to James.

"What brings you to the Highlands, old friend?"

"I learned from a well-meaning source that you were going to attend the London Season. Why, for the love of God, would you do such a thing?" James dropped down into the chair opposite Ioan and sighed. "You're a duke now and considered quite a catch. Your name is already in the betting book at White's. The mamas are circling. It's a trap, I tell you. *A trap.*"

Ioan chuckled briefly, the sound almost foreign to him after being in a melancholy state for so long after...he decided he better stop himself there.

"My father had a contact at Whitehall that may shine some light on what happened to him and my brothers. It's the only clue I've got. Whitehall is in London; therefore, I must go to London." Ioan stood, strode to the nearby decanters, and poured two fingers of brandy in each of the two glasses. He handed one to James as he made his way back to his desk.

"Ioan, my oldest and dearest friend, your days of being a rake of the highest order are gone for good." James rolled his eyes and laughed.

"I am assuming that you mean to travel with me to London?" Ioan smirked.

"If I must, I must." His friend took a sip of the brandy.

James' head then snapped up. "The Season starts in four weeks. We better start sooner rather than later. Lucky for you, I brought my ship. When my parents died, they left me their shares of a shipping company located in Plymouth."

"I wasn't planning on traveling so soon. Let me ring Jeffers—"

The man appeared suddenly in the doorway. "Your Grace, I had a footman and your valet start packing for your journey to London. Your trunks are ready and the carriages have been prepared for your departure. Safe travels, Your Grace."

"How does he do that?" James asked as he finished his drink.

"I wish I could tell you." Ioan took one last sip of his brandy.

"Shall we be off?" Ioan stood up and crossed the room to the door while beckoning his friend to join him.

James smiled roguishly. "Let's go set the *Ton* on fire with our escapades. What do you say? One last hurrah before we meet the marriage noose?"

As Ioan left the room, he listened to the laughter of his friend and experienced a renewed hope that everything was going to be all right in the end.

Chapter Two

London, England
Two weeks later

IOAN HAD SETTLED into his townhouse in Mayfair, enjoying the peace around him. He knew—eventually—that peace would be disrupted by the chaos of callers, friends, and the upper echelons of the English peerage.

He settled into one of the chairs in the parlor, nestling a steaming cup of tea in his hands, taking a sip of the hot brew while staring into the fire; the orange glow of the flames seemed to relax him.

It was in this moment that he was reminded of how unprepared he was for coming into the London Season. His valet was beyond exasperated with him for his lack of evening wear. Since arriving in London, Ioan had procured an appointment at a tailor to have a wardrobe fit for his station made.

A tap on the door alerted him to a footman's presence. "Your Grace, the carriage is ready for you."

If he must—he must. "Very well. Thank you, Oliver."

The footman, Oliver, bowed and left the room. Ioan placed his tea cup on the small table beside his chair and rose to his feet. It was time to brave the outside world for a time.

Ioan couldn't believe it! Every young woman along his route from his tailor to his club—a membership he inherited—tried to launch themselves into his arms. A couple young women "fainted" at his feet. Another stepped across the road, just to be nearly hit by an oncoming carriage. Yet another fell out of her carriage, ruining her gown on the way down.

He rolled his eyes as he strode into the club, seeking a bit of solitude before braving the wilds once more. As he found an empty chair, an older man joined him. The man was dressed fashionably, his dark hair pulled back in a cue.

"It has been a while since we've met. I am your father's friend, Lord Tarleton." The man held out his hand.

Ioan grabbed the proffered hand and shook it before taking a seat, and motioned Tarleton to do the same in the chair next to his. "What can I do for you, my lord?" he asked in confusion.

"Your father and elder brothers were working on a project for me before their deaths. I have a feeling that they were murdered because of what they found."

"I was not privy to their personal lives, other than what they wanted me to know. I found some notes in a locked drawer in a desk in the study, but nothing that made sense."

"Do you remember anything from those notes?" Tarleton asked in a commanding tone.

"Of course I do. I can remember everything I read—it's a curse, if you ask me," Ioan replied.

"I would like you to join me at my office at Whitehall to discuss what you remember. I may need your help to solve this case."

Whitehall? What am I getting myself into? he asked himself. He had never heard of Tarleton. He had never heard that his family had been in the business of spying. It would make a bit of sense. He had friends who were part of a hereditary spy network known as the Knights of Justice. Maybe his family had been too?

"I am willing to speak with you about what I know."

"I will send you a missive with the date and time. I am thinking—the sooner, the better—don't you think? How about tomorrow?" Tarleton asked.

Ioan nodded. "I will write that down once I get home. Which reminds me, I must be on my way." Ioan pushed himself off the chair and stood, shaking Tarleton's hand again, and strode off.

LADY MATILDA WALSH was late again—she was perpetually late. The large grandfather clock that stood sentry in the main hall of her father's London townhouse chimed—if one could call it that, since it sounded more like the bells of St. George's and not that of a clock—the three o'clock hour.

She was supposed to meet her cousin Eudora at the modiste. Matilda sighed as she rushed out the door, down the stairs, and almost lost her footing on the last step—almost. A rather large, moving object with auburn hair stopped her fall. The object, it was surely no object but a man, didn't just stop her fall, but broke it before she could reach the end of the walk. Luckily for her, she didn't fall *into* her awaiting carriage. She fell on top of the man.

"If it isn't ladies swooning, it's ladies falling into me. For the love of Mary and Joseph, please get off me." The man's baritone voice penetrated her addled mind.

"Oh. I'm so sorry." She clambered to right herself, yet somehow, she ended up not moving a single inch. "I am so clumsy. I tripped—"

"Please, don't," the man ground out. "Just get off of me without kneeing me—"

Well, that had not worked out the way that she thought it would. As she lifted herself onto all fours, two things happened: one, her knee must have come down on a rather unfortunate place of the man's anatomy. Two, her elbow connected with the place between his ribs and his diaphragm, causing a whoosh of air to escape from his lips.

There was nothing for it, she couldn't do much more damage than she already had. She quickly pushed herself the rest of the way up until she was standing peering down at her—savior? She didn't know what else to call him. She hadn't planned on tripping down the stairs and falling into a man, a rather handsome one. She had to get her thoughts together.

"I'm sor—"

"Enough, please. Whatever excuse you were going to tell me, just don't. I've heard it all ever since I decided to come back to London. I just want to be left alone—but no." The man finally groaned as he pushed himself up from the ground.

"Sir—"

"Please, my lady, let me help you to the carriage and hope that all will go well," the man sighed.

She couldn't help the smile that spread across her face until she remembered where she had to be and that her cousin was waiting at the modiste with her footman—alone. She needed to get to her carriage quickly if she was going to be unfashionably late to her appointment.

"There is no need for your assistance, sir. I am sorry—again."

The man nodded and strode down the sidewalk.

IOAN COULDN'T BELIEVE what had happened. He was on his way back to his townhouse in Mayfair when he, quite literally, stumbled upon the young lady that he had run into. He rolled his eyes towards the heavens and sighed. It could have been much worse—much, much worse. Was this going to be a daily ritual? Ioan hoped that it wasn't. He was a duke of marriageable age, he was rather handsome, if he said so himself—and he was rich. Three items on the minds of every single young lady and her exasperating mama.

The young lady that he had stumbled into seemed to not realize who he was—which was unbelievable. He shook his head at his good fortune. He couldn't wrap his mind around that.

Almost everyone knew that he was the Duke of Rathdrum. If they didn't, the introductions at the many social events he had been invited to had proved otherwise.

Ioan strode up the limestone stairs to his townhouse and closed the door on the world. Hoping for a couple of moments of uninterrupted peace.

"Your Grace, you have a visitor. He has been waiting—impatiently—for the last couple of hours while awaiting your return," his butler, who he couldn't remember the name of, spoke through clenched teeth.

"Oh? Show him to my study and I will meet him that presently." Ioan threaded his fingers through his hair. He couldn't believe his luck.

"Very well, Your Grace." The butler bowed and turned down the hall toward the parlor.

Ioan must have done something horrible in a past life—if he believed in past lives—to get this sort of punishment. Ioan heard the *tap, tap, tap* of shoes clacking over the marble flooring. He let out a sigh, wishing he was anywhere but where he was. He didn't look back before he marched into his study—moments before the butler, with his visitor, entered the room.

Ioan's mouth dropped open.

"It has been a long time, my friend." Phineas Stanton sketched a bow.

Ioan had missed spending time with his mischievous friend. Finn, as his friends called him, was always getting into one scrape or another—mostly to do with the opposite sex. Ioan pulled his friend into an embrace.

"There is no need to bow. We've been friends for years. What brings you to my door?"

"A little birdy—ahem, James—told me you were in town. Not just James, Ioan, but the entire *Ton* is buzzing with gossip about you. My little sister, you remember Lizzie, she was spouting all sorts of interesting gossip."

Ioan shook his head. He should have known that London

would be atwitter about his appearance in town—months after deaths of his family. "To be frank, I'm surprised that the gossips haven't moved on to a person more scandalous than me."

"More scandalous than you? Who is more scandalous? You used to be London's premier rakehell," Finn laughed.

"That was the old me. All I want now is peace and quiet, but from the looks of things—I am not going to get it since every marriageable young maid is throwing herself at me," Ioan replied while rolling his eyes.

"Didn't James tell you that you were the most illegible bachelor this Season? You want peace? You should have stayed in the highlands." Finn collapsed onto the settee in the parlor and stretched out.

Finn couldn't have said anything more true. If only he didn't feel the urge to find the person who took the lives of his father and brothers. He needed to apprehend the murderer himself—maybe, with the help of Lord Tarleton. That sparked a thought. Maybe Finn knew of the man.

"I was visited by a man at my club—a Lord Tarleton. Do you know him?"

"Do I know the man? Yes. He is the man in charge of all His Majesty's informants—spies. I work for him. This must be about a project that your family was doing for Tarleton?"

"He certainly thinks so. I am not so sure. I speak with him more tomorrow at his office at Whitehall."

"Be prepared. He may try to recruit you to the cause." Finn chortled.

Ioan rolled his eyes. "I have enough to worry about—I have no time for spy games."

"Have you been invited to the Haversham Ball?"

Ioan couldn't help the laugh that escaped his lips. "Yes, and I plan on going."

"Tarleton will be appearing with his goddaughter tonight. He may try to speak with you there—if you aren't being hounded by the dragons and the infernal mamas of the *Ton*."

Ioan nodded. He had one suit of eveningwear that he could use—if all went well, he would be able to catch the person before a threat to his bachelorhood would come for him.

Chapter Three

MATILDA THOUGHT BACK on the day as she dressed for the Haversham Ball. Her godfather would be her escort to the most sought after invite of the Season. She didn't want to go, but if she was going to snare a husband, it was a necessary evil. Luckily, she made her appointment with her cousin at the modiste. The final fitting on the evening's gown of choice had been an easy affair.

The gown was a beautiful shade of blue with gold cording throughout. The empire waist helped accentuate her figure—not that there was much there, yet it helped. The blue, more a lavender than blue, complemented her mahogany brown hair and brought out the blue of her eyes. She fell in love with the gown—again.

She felt the ever present presence of her lady's maid staring at her.

"My lady, you are beautiful. What would you like me to do with your hair?"

"A chignon with tendrils of curls framing my face—simple, yet elegant." Matilda smiled.

Alice nodded and went to work on Matilda's hair.

"All done, my lady. Anything more I can do for you before you go on your way?"

"No, Alice. That will be all for tonight. Enjoy the rest of your night; you deserve it," Matilda pushed herself up from where she had been sitting while Alice had been doing her hair.

"You best not tarry for long, my lady. Lord Tarleton arrived not long ago," a footman said from the door of her rooms as she strode passed him.

"Would you tell him that I will be down presently?" she asked the footman as she continued down the hall towards the room that used to be her mother's.

Though her mother had died when Matilda was six years old, her presence could always be felt in the room that had been hers. Matilda had made sure that her mother's jewels never left the house—and kept them in the only room her father would never enter—her mother's room. She marched herself over to the small vault that housed the original jewels that her mother had come to her marriage with. The sapphire earbobs and matching necklace would complement her ensemble very well.

She took the jewels from the vault and quickly made her way downstairs to the parlor—where she knew Uncle Tarleton would be waiting impatiently for her. She turned into the room and noticed the beautiful suit of eveningwear that Tarleton had on.

"Uncle, you are looking handsome tonight," she said as he bowed to her.

Anthony Farrington, Lord Tarleton, was fifteen years her senior, her mother's youngest brother. He had been granted a title by Prinny, the Prince Regent, for services rendered to the Crown. The man was more a brother than an uncle—yet her parents made him her godfather. She supposed that it was in good taste that her parents did such a thing. She didn't know if her uncle had been in the business—what she called his occupation— at the time or not, but she was thankful, nonetheless.

"You, my darling girl, are as beautiful as ever." The man grinned.

"Thank you, uncle!" She twirled in place as if she transported herself back into her childhood.

"When we are out and about, my darling, you will need to call me your godfather. Most of the *Ton* doesn't remember—

strangely—that I am your uncle. I would prefer to keep that way because of the work I do for the Crown," he admonished her.

"I understand. You don't want me to be more of a target than I already am." Matilda confirmed her suspicions.

Her uncle nodded. "Yes, among other reasons. As a ward, you are a target—but, as my niece, you are infinitely more so. I've lost my sister, I have no desire to lose you, my darling."

The butler padded across the room to announce that the carriage was ready for them. Matilda nodded. This wasn't her first ball, yet she was anxious about it. She was, for all it was worth, a glorified wallflower.

Yes, her uncle—the eyes and ears of the Crown—cast his horrific gaze toward any suitor that came to call. Horrific? Where did that word come from? Not that he wasn't handsome— because he was…very handsome—it was that look. The one that threatened infinite torture, fire and brimstone, and every unpleasant punishment known to man if any of the young lords put a single finger on her.

How was she supposed to find a husband? She knew what her uncle was up to. The gentleman that would be her husband would not be scared off by her uncle's surly glances. She couldn't help but smile at his antics.

"…here's your…"

Matilda mentally shook herself from her musings. She managed to catch part of what her uncle was saying when she saw the cloak that he held in his arms. She took a deep breath and turned away from him so that he could put the cloak around her shoulders and help her to the awaiting carriage.

The carriage line for the front entry to Haversham House was quite a bit longer than Matilda had expected. She glanced out of the window of the coach to find they had maybe twenty carriages in front of them. This was going to be a bigger affair than the previous year. With Parliament in session, more notable men and women had come to town. When the upper echelons of the British nobility made an appearance, there was more and more need for entertainment.

Matilda had gotten a missive from her cousin—the very same one that she had nearly missed the appointment with—that the Scottish Duke of Rathdrum would be making an appearance. She had met the Duke of Rathdrum once before. He was an older man with a thick Scots brogue. Why her cousin would be excited for such a man, she had no inclination, nor had the intention to be introduced to him once again. She dismissed her cousin's excitement.

Stuck in her head, Matilda felt the carriage jerk to a halt. She blinked and glanced out the window to see the massive oak doors of Haversham House. Time had, once again, skipped forward. The door opened as she saw the face of a footman in Haversham livery, extending his arm to help her alight from the carriage.

Matilda smiled at the footman and waited for her uncle to escort her into the house.

The Haversham Ball was a lavish affair—bouquets of flowers, candles lighting up the ballroom, and a beautiful water feature in the garden. Lady Haversham was a matchmaker of sorts. She enjoyed watching the young lords and ladies find love—and if that meant having her garden open to public during her ball, she would do so. The string quartet, tuning their instruments, was in the alcove above the dance floor. She smiled to herself. The opulence of the room, the glittering of the chandelier, the elegantly dressed lords and ladies—she held in a breath in awe of it all.

"Darling, I have someone I would like to introduce you to," her uncle said, bringing her out of her own thoughts.

Matilda nodded. She held on to her uncle's arm as he guided her through the throng of people. In one of the far corners of the ballroom, she noticed a man—not just any man, the one she accidentally ran into—surrounded by several other gentlemen. *Damn and blast!* she said to herself. She glanced up at the man. Their eyes met—and held.

"Uncle, who is that man in the corner?" She tilted her head in the man's direction.

She watched as her uncle perused the room. "The gentleman with the auburn hair? That is His Grace, the Duke of Rathdrum."

Matilda had never been as shocked, except at the death of her parents. The horrors of it all. It never occurred to her that she had assaulted a duke. She felt mortified. Her eyes dropped to the floor. Her life as she knew it had ended. She knew that the duke would punish her for her mistake earlier that day.

Her uncle brought her out of her thoughts by saying, "I am going to introduce you to him—"

⁕

Chapter Four

OUT OF ALL the ladies Ioan wanted to avoid, his eyes happened to collide with the one who damaged his pride on a sidewalk. What made it worse? She was on the arm of Lord Tarleton—and they were making their way to him. It was much too late to make an early departure. He would have to withstand the onslaught. He bolstered himself by taking a deep breath and joined his hands behind his back.

"Your Grace, it is good to see you. Are you enjoying the ball?" Lord Tarleton asked.

"I have been, my lord. It has been entertaining—" was all that he could think of to say. Truth be told, he was unsure why he was at the party.

"Your Grace, I would like to introduce you to my goddaughter, Lady Matilda Walsh."

Ioan took Matilda's hand, the one that wasn't occupied by holding onto her godfather's arm, and bowed over it—placing a platonic kiss on the top of her hand. He stared into her eyes as he did so. Her hand was warm in his, even through their gloves. He was struck with the intensity of her gaze.

"A pleasure, my lady. Do you have any dances left?" Ioan asked as he lifted Matilda's dance card where it hung on her wrist and scribbled his name for the first waltz. He wanted to speak with her, and the alcoves—for obvious reasons—were not the place to do so, especially with her uncle guarding her. He raised her hand to his lips again. "Until our dance, my lady." He nodded at Lord Tarleton.

Ioan shocked himself. Earlier in the day, he had been frustrated and angry over all the women throwing themselves at him. He took out that frustration on an innocent woman. What better than a waltz to help clear the air? He didn't want an error in judgment to cause a rift. He felt something for the girl. He didn't want to examine that too closely, especially since he just met her a few hours earlier.

Ioan shook his head.

"What was that?" James asked from behind him.

"I was introduced to a young lady." Ioan turned to step away from the men in his inner circle—if one could call it that.

"I saw that part. There is a story there, *Your Grace,* and as your friend, I want to know what that is." James placed his hands on his hips, mimicking the stance of a dowager countess nearby.

Ioan couldn't hold back the laughter—which was a social faux pas. He was a duke, though, and thought that—maybe—he would be able to have a bit of leeway.

Apparently, because of the hushed tones in the ballroom, he wasn't given that little courtesy. He had not even noticed that the orchestra had quit tuning their instruments, as well. Then the call for the waltz had been announced.

Ioan searched through the crowded ballroom for Matilda—and locked eyes with her. She was standing with her godfather, clinging to his arm. In his rush toward her, he nearly trampled on an unsuspecting couple and an older man that he had forgotten the name of. He glanced up to find Matilda's eyes shining with laughter, as he watched her cover her face with her fan. He couldn't help but chuckle a bit to himself.

He finally reached her. "My lady, I believe this is our dance." Ioan took her hand once more and brushed a kiss across the top of it.

"I believe you are right," she replied as she glanced down at her dance card.

Ioan smiled down at her. "Shall we?"

As they strode to the dance floor, Ioan kept quiet—not knowing what to say. The orchestra started to play a waltz, and like they were meant to dance together, Ioan was pleasantly surprised how well in-tune Matilda was with his dance steps.

"My lady—" he started.

"Please, call me Matilda, or Maddy. I don't like formality unless I don't have a choice."

"Very well." He caught himself before using her title. "Matilda, I want to apologize for earlier. I was short with you. I had a terrible day and I took that frustration out on you.

"You have been forgiven."

What an amazing young lady, he spoke to himself. If he was in the market for a wife, he would be happy with Matilda, but he wasn't, as it were, and likely would never be. Life had prepared him for the inevitable, and he would despise himself if what happened to his family…happened to him.

Ioan continued to dip and swirl around the ballroom with Matilda in his arms.

"Your Grace, my cousin and I were contemplating why you were here for the Season if you weren't seeking a wife—"

"*Tsk, tsk*, my lady. Has anyone advised you not to listen to gossip?" He smiled down at her. He knew the question would come sooner or later. He just had hoped that he could go a bit longer without it being asked.

"I do not, Your Grace. Well, only if my cousin reads the news sheets. There is so much that isn't written about. I can always ask my godfather. He would tell me." Matilda smiled back at him with mischief in her eyes.

There was more to the woman than he originally thought. "My father and two older brothers died six months back. At first, everyone thought that it was an accident. Our family doctor notated the condition of the bodies and had written that there was foam coming out of their mouths. That wasn't bad food. That was poison."

"Weren't you there?" Matilda asked.

"No." He shook his head as they neared another couple. "I was in Edinburgh when they died."

"Oh!" She gasped.

The music stopped and Ioan spun Matilda to a standstill—and sketched a bow. "My lady, I hope to dance with you again soon." And he walked away.

Matilda stood staring after Ioan as he strode through the crowded room. She could barely catch her breath as she sought her uncle. She felt out of sorts. She was jittery with excitement. Her heart raced just thinking of the dance they had. She didn't know for certain, but she was sure that she was blushing. What was wrong with her? She chided herself. She caught her uncle's eyes and hurried to him.

"Can we leave?" she asked, hoping that he didn't want to stay any longer.

"We can, but let me speak with one of my men first."

Matilda nodded. She knew there was a reason why her uncle was at this ball—her father. Any other Season, her father could have been found in the gambling room, designated for those who didn't want to dance. This Season, there was no sign of her godforsaken parent. There was something going on, and she was determined to ascertain what that was.

She waited impatiently as her uncle crossed the room to speak with one of the men that had been in Rathdrum's presence when she had walked into the ball. The man was one of her uncle's men. She recognized him since she was closer. Phineas Stanton. Of course, he had come to Tarelton House many times when she was there. He had always been nice to her—well, as nice as he could be to a girl who found herself in scrapes of one sort or another. To think on it, she was still getting herself into scrapes.

"Shall we depart these hallowed halls, my dear?"

Matilda nodded. She took her godfather's proffered arm and left the ball.

Chapter Five

THE NEXT MORNING, Ioan sat behind his desk with a quill in hand. He had spent all night writing down everything he remembered seeing at his father's desk at Rathdrum Hall. His near perfect memory did not disappoint. He remembered everything down to the minute scrap on the polished wood.

The one thing he forgot was sleep. How could one forget to sleep? It wasn't as if his mind was inactive—because it was, very active. He pushed himself up from his chair and stretched. The pain in his upper back and shoulders was testament of how he spent his night—crouched over a desk, writing—in the dark, with a candle for light.

He glanced at himself in the mirror above the mantle of the fireplace. *Good God!* He looked like hell warmed over. His once slicked back hair had been mussed so many times that he looked like a ragamuffin. He held back a chuckle at his own appearance. He combed his fingers through his hair to put it to right. He took another glance in the mirror and nodded. He was put together enough to have an appointment with Tarleton.

He waited a moment before tugging on the bellpull—forgetting that he was in the London townhouse, not Rathdrum Hall.

"Your Grace?"

"Have a carriage brought around, I have an appointment at Whitehall." He paced back and forth behind his desk.

"Very well, Your Grace. Shall I have Morrison come down, as well?"

Ioan supposed that having Morrison, his valet, help him tame his unruly hair may be a good idea. "Yes, I will need Morrison, and have him bring a change of attire, also."

The footman nodded, a bow and hurried from the room.

Ioan glanced down at the pages and pages of handwritten notes that he had spent all night putting together and sighed. He was exhausted emotionally, physically—mentally. If it wasn't the morning of his appointment with Tarleton, he would cancel it until he was well rested enough to think. Unfortunately, that was not something he could do.

He groaned and rubbed his eyes as his valet strode into the study with a fresh set of clothes and grooming supplies.

⇉⤜⫷

IOAN FOUND HIMSELF walking in the dark hallways of Whitehall—trying to find the spy master's office. Then it dawned on him. Several doors back, a soldier guarded a door. He pivoted on his feet and strode back toward the soldier.

"Is this Lord Tarleton's office?" Ioan asked.

"It may be, Your Grace." The guard stared at Ioan. "Do you have an appointment?"

Ioan smiled mischievously. "Of course I have a bloody appointment."

The guard stepped aside and smiled back—motioning for Ioan to enter the room.

Of course, being the gentleman his mother taught him to be, Ioan knocked on the door. He stood there, staring at the door for several minutes. Nothing. He knocked again. Nothing. He glanced back at the guard and noticed the smile on the other man's face.

"Let me guess—I need to let myself in—"

The guard nodded and motioned, yet again, to the door.

Ioan sighed as he turned the doorknob and opened the door. He peeked into the room and saw the spy master staring at a book in front of him with a frown on his face. At that moment, Ioan wished that he had canceled the appointment for the day.

"Please, have a seat, Your Grace." The man kept staring at the book.

"How did you know it was me?" Ioan couldn't help but ask.

"You have a very distinct gait. I knew you were on your way here before you knew where my office was. Plus, I like to test all my friends and cohorts." Tarleton smiled. "I, also, couldn't help but test you even further to see if you would come into my office without permission. From now on, walk in. I will tell the guard if that changes."

Ioan nodded his head.

"Now, Your Grace, let's see the notes that you have on what you saw in your father's study—" Tarleton finally glanced up at him.

Ioan handed over his notes with a smile and relished the feeling that he was going to surprise the spy master with his memory. He watched keenly has the older man read through the stack of vellum that Ioan had handed him.

⟫⟫⟫✦⟪⟪⟪

AN HOUR HAD passed since Ioan had handed his notes over to the spy master. The man had occasionally asked questions, but much of the time, he had flipped through the pages. Ioan's skin was crawling with the need to do something. *Damn and blast*, he yelled to himself.

"You do have a knack for detail, Your Grace. I could use your skills in my line of work. With your family's records, I think we can put this mystery to rest." The spy master glanced up at Ioan.

There was an uneasiness that crept under his skin. Why

would the spy master bring up the family records?

"I know that questioning look well. Your father and brothers had the same expressions on their faces when I brought up the family records. You see, except for the Doomsday Book, your family has the most extensive library of documents about families and lineages throughout the Continent. Your family was doing some research on a specific surname for me when they died—" Tarleton responded.

Ioan couldn't believe what he was hearing. He knew that his family records were extensive, but he hadn't realized that they were *that* extensive. His ancestors had rescued some of the church records before the protestant kings—predominately King Henry VIII—could pilfer them or even destroy them.

"I see that this is a surprise to you, Your Grace. I would like your help with this project. If you choose to proceed, I have some men under my command that I would have work with you. In fact, you may know these men. I will grant you a sennight to decide." The spy master stared at Ioan and then dismissed him by going back to whatever he had been reading before being interrupted.

Ioan pulled himself from the chair he had been sitting in and strode to the door. He had a lot to think about—or did he really? He could finish what they had started and, in doing so, could potentially find their killer.

Chapter Six

Somewhere in the slums of London

WHEN HE WAS a young man, he never thought that his life would take the pivotal turn that it had. Just like any young man with means, his father sent him to school. He was given a title. He had younger brothers and sisters. It was a shock to him when he found out that he was a…

He was a bastard. A by-blow. His married father had duped some little debutante and got her with child. It had been several years since he had learned of the secret—and that's what finally pushed him over the edge. In other words, his soul turned dark and he made it his mission in life to ruin his father's name.

That's how he found himself inside a rundown tavern amid the slums. His informant, by the glancing at his watch, was late—again. He rolled his eyes and sighed. The man was always late. He surveyed the room, taking in the faces of the men—and women—surrounding him. Of course, he was also watching for his contact.

"Sir? A missive has arrived." The owner of the tavern handed him the note and walked away.

Mr. Black,

I have been detained. I will be at the appointed place late.

Yours,

Mr. Grey

He glanced down at his watch again. He was beyond upset with this godforsaken imbecile. He needed information, and *Mr. Grey* was the only man that he got *somewhat* valuable information from. He slammed his fist onto the table where he sat. Mr. Grey would pay for this. Pay for the wasted time he was forced to endure. He let his temper simmer, banking his need to smash his fist into someone—anyone's face.

Mr. Black, as he was called, searched the tavern—again. If he stayed in the tavern for too long, he would be at risk of being discovered. Being what he was, being discovered could prove detrimental to his health—he knew what the Crown did to those who were caught spying against them.

Mr. Grey would live to see another day—and Mr. Black was not happy about that. He had superior instincts, and they told him that Mr. Grey was not who he portrayed himself to be.

LORD PERCY WALSH had, in fact, been detained—by his late wife's brother, his boss. Tarleton had worried that Percy's disguise had been compromised. He had known that Matilda would eventually catch on. She was so preceptive. Not to mention that her uncle—godfather—had taught her a couple of things over the years. Percy was not thrilled that his wife's brother would teach Matilda some of their trade.

He sat down into the chair behind his desk, completely forgetting that Tarleton was berating him from the other side.

"...*how dare you!*"

Percy glanced up to Tarleton's face. "Do you think I had a choice? Mr. Black is catching on to the fact that I am not who I claim to be. It's getting dangerous enough for me to pass on the information to him without getting caught myself."

"Have I not taught you anything over the years? You know

what you need to do, my lord. I should have been informed months ago, when your instincts told you that you were found out. *Goddamn it!*" Tarleton stormed up to the desk and threw his fists down. "Don't you know how this can affect Matilda?"

"Of course I know how this could affect my daughter. She already suspects something. It's all your fault that you taught her some of our craft. I still don't understand why you did that." Percy rose from his chair and placed his hands on the desk.

"Matilda has an astute gift. She needed to be challenged and I gave her that challenge, with my sister's approval," Tarleton retorted.

Percy couldn't argue with that. Matilda had outgrown her tutor and her nanny's knowledge by the time she was seven years old. His late wife would have done anything to occupy their daughter, even if that was learning additional languages, codes, and puzzles. Yet, he couldn't quite get over the fact that she was in as much danger as he was.

"Why do you think I settled you and Matilda in the old safehouse? That was me trying to keep you and her safe. You are one of our greatest assets—same with Matilda. The Crown cannot afford to lose either one of you."

Percy mulled what Tarleton said over and over in his mind. He was irreplaceable. Tarleton knew how to get him to calm down, the bastard.

"It's too late now to go to the meeting place. I will have to reschedule the meet." Percy strode around the desk.

He knew what he needed to do and he would need to be more cautious. He needed to make plans, escape plans. He would need contingency plans for Matilda in case something happened to him.

"Oh, and Percy—" Tarleton *hmph*ed. "A certain Scottish duke seems to think that you have something to do with the deaths of his family. You may want to have a conversation with him as soon as you can before he tries to have you arrested."

Percy grimaced. He knew he would have to speak with the

Duke of Rathdrum sooner rather than later. He was just not ready for that. Maybe, just maybe, a moment would present itself to him. He smiled to himself. He needed to focus on his mission, not on personal matters.

He sat down, once again, at his desk and wrote a missive to Mr. Black—stating that he could no longer keep his appointment and asked if they could meet in a couple of days in a more lucrative location. He yanked on the bellpull and waited for a footman to answer his call.

He knew what he did was dangerous, but Tarleton had made sure that Matilda, his light in the darkness, would never have to deal with the aftermath of his profession.

"My lord?" a footman said from the door.

"Give this to the boy and see that he comes back with a reply." Percy handed the missive to the footman, hoping that all would be right.

※ ❖ ※

Chapter Seven

I OAN SAT AT his desk, thinking about the meeting that he had with the spy master. The man had offered him a place with the Crown. The issue with working with Tarleton was he didn't choose his own missions. He needed that control. Then an idea took root in his mind—and he smiled. He didn't want to be a spy; he wanted to bring thieves and murderers to justice. The Bow Street Runners were good, but he wanted his own project.

The more he thought about the idea, the more he liked it. He still needed to learn everything he could from the spy master about investigating and reading clues. Ioan had a few friends he could turn to—James and Phineas were two that came to mind. James was in the Scottish Dragoons, while Phineas worked with the damn spy master.

Ioan reached for a quill and vellum—and started writing. First, he wrote out his plans for the investigative service. Second, he wrote missives to his friends for a meeting at his townhouse. He would only hire the most honorable and valorous of men— those who fought on the Continent and needed work. An idea of what he would call it came to mind: Of Valor and Honor Investigative Service.

He would still work alongside Tarleton, making it easier for the man to put all his resources into intelligence and intrigue. Where Ioan could investigate the crime angle. He glanced up at the picture of his father above the fireplace. His father would be proud of him; he knew it instinctively. He would find whoever murdered his family and he would find whoever ordered the man to do so.

Ioan reached behind him and yanked on the bellpull, waiting for a footman to answer his call. While waiting, he folded the vellum and sealed both missives with his family seal.

"Your Grace?" A footman answered as he crossed the room.

"I would like you to deliver these missives posthaste and with the most urgency. Oh, and please, wait for the reply." Ioan handed over the missives and bid the footman to be on his way.

WHILE AWAITING THE replies from James and Phineas, Ioan decided upon a visit to his neighbor. It had been several days since he had seen Matilda. He could never determine whether she was going to be in a facetious mood or a belligerent one. Hopefully, it would be the latter. He enjoyed the repartee they had. He glanced in the mirror adjacent to the fireplace and deemed himself presentable. Ioan took up his walking stick, the one with a lion's face on it and a stiletto hidden in the handle, and strode toward Matilda's townhouse.

The butler opened the door to him and ushered Ioan in. The sound of music wafted through the halls.

"My lady is quite the musician, Your Grace. She is working through something. You can tell by what she is playing." The butler strode on.

The haunting strains of Beethoven's "Moonlight Sonata" found their way to his ears as Ioan followed the butler to the library where a beautiful piano forte was set out. Matilda swayed with the music. Ioan couldn't take his eyes off her. If the butler was correct, she was working through something tragic by the sounds of the piece.

Ioan had heard the lesser known sonata—preferring Mozart's

sonatas—before, but never heard it played like Matilda was playing it. She played with such emotion. Ioan could feel tears well up in his eyes, threatening to spill at any time. Matilda had a way with the piano forte—and he couldn't look away.

Just as the sonata finished, she changed to a waltz. The butler sighed. "She has made her decision and it's a happy one, Your Grace."

Ioan could've told the butler that just by the happy smile that was now secure on her face. He nodded and stood watching as she played the joyful tune. As it ended, she finally turned her face towards him. Never in all his years had he witnessed such a performance.

"Your Grace, I wasn't expecting you." She stood from the bench she had been perched on.

Ioan bowed. "Lady Matilda, I was done with my appointments for the day and thought about visiting before the hordes of lords swamp your parlor."

"If only, Your Grace. My godfather scares most of the lords off at the ball. He believes that there is no one good enough for me." Matilda smiled.

"Your godfather is truly an intimidating force of nature, my lady," Ioan replied. He had experience now with Tarleton, and the man was indeed a force unto himself.

"That he is, Your Grace."

Ioan was in awe of the woman in front of him. She was truly magnificent—talented, intelligent, and beautiful.

"How may I be of assistance to you, Your Grace?" she asked as she approached him, hand outstretched.

Ioan took her hand and brought it up to his lips for a chaste kiss to the back of it. Ioan flushed at her question, though. What was he doing here? "I—well—was thinking about you..." Ioan couldn't finish that sentence without sounding as if he was stuttering.

Matilda giggled. "Your Grace, I do appreciate you visiting me today. Would you mind following me to the parlor—my lady's maid will be down shortly to chaperone."

Ioan followed her as they made it through the maze of halls to get to the parlor. He was amazed at the house. Though it was the same exterior as his home, the space inside was deceptive.

Ioan couldn't make sense of the differences. The rooms were smaller. He searched his memory for the history of the house— but came up with nothing.

"Do you know anything about the history of this house?" he asked as they came to the parlor.

"The house has been in my family for generations. It is currently owned by my uncle—my mother's younger brother," she replied, not skipping a beat.

Ioan was utterly shocked that she would disclose the history. He could admit that he knew a bit about the house. From what his father said when he was younger, the house had been a meeting place for Catholics during the Reformation. He did not know, though, that the house was owned by Matilda's family.

"I would not normally tell someone I just met about this house. I saw the shocked look on your face. As our neighbor and because you had a meeting with the owner of this house, I believed that I could disclose certain histories. Unless, I am sadly mistaken. Am I mistaken, Your Grace?" She cocked her eyebrow at him.

Ioan couldn't hold back the chuckle any longer. "You are not mistaken, my lady."

"As I thought." Matilda nodded.

"...wait, your uncle owns this house? I had a meeting with him?"

Ioan watched as a myriad of emotions flitted through her eyes.

"Well, yes—"

"Tarleton is your uncle," Ioan stated. He had not expected that twist. Well, damn. That would explain a lot. He mentally shook himself. He glanced over at Matilda to see her nodding.

"In public, he is just my godfather for my safety." She motioned for him to take a seat.

Ioan could understand needing his loved ones to be safe. Though, wouldn't any of the numerous marriageable young ladies know deBretts frontward and backward? Those ladies would surely know of Lady Matilda and Lord Tarleton's relationship.

As if Matilda knew where his thoughts were taking him, she said," Your Grace, my mother was not a peer of the realm, nor was she a member of the gentry. Her brother, by a different father, was—though, his title was awarded him because of the work he has done for the Crown."

Ioan ached to get his fingers on his family's records. He needed to figure out this mystery—among many.

"Thank you, my lady, for entrusting me with this knowledge and know that I will not break your confidence."

MATILDA DIDN'T MEAN to tell the duke so much. In fact, she was sure that her uncle would have plenty to say about it when she would tell him about her mistake. She cringed at the thought.

"Your Grace, I have an appointment soon and I don't want to be late. If you don't mind, I would like to continue this conversation later."

Who was she fooling? She was perpetually late, given the fact that she made up said appointment—she groaned to herself. There was always the fact that she couldn't lie to save her life. Apparently, the overly handsome man in front of her could read her better than her uncle could.

"My lady, I will let myself out. Before I do, I would ask if you would like to go on a curricle ride through Hyde Park tomorrow?"

Matilda couldn't believe her ears and merely nodded her head in agreement.

"Then, I will see you on the morrow," the duke said as he pushed himself out of his chair and ambled out the door.

Matilda couldn't wrap her mind around what just happened in her parlor. Well, she would need to write a note to Uncle Anthony explaining her faux pa. She strolled to her father's study—pulled out a piece of vellum and a quill out of the left hand drawer of her father's desk, and set out to write her uncle a missive.

Chapter Eight

MATILDA WAS NOT accustomed to upsetting her uncle, and the scene that had occurred after she sent a footman to deliver her letter—needless to say, Uncle Anthony was livid. Well, she supposed it could have gone much worse—much worse. She had gone to her secret room that she had found after the move to this house, the one with the piano.

She remembered that day like it was yesterday. She was in the music room and noticed a bookshelf. One of the books—a Shakespeare tome—was slightly off kilter. When she pushed the book to slide it the rest of the way into the shelf, she heard a soft *click*.

It surprised her when the whole bookshelf opened into a secret room. Clearly, it was soundproof because—inside the secret room was a piano forte. Knowing what the house used to be, it shouldn't have surprised her that there were secret rooms and passageways.

Ever since, Matilda composed her own music in secret. In the compartment inside the piano bench, she had several finished compositions. One day, possibly, she would perform them in front of an audience—though, lady musicians were frowned upon. Or she had even thought about publishing them under an assumed name. Yet, she couldn't stand for someone to get the credit for her work.

Thinking back to that day made her curious. She glanced

around her father's study—surveying the floor-to-ceiling bookcases. It was then she noticed the book—another Shakespeare tome. It was sticking out of its space on the shelf.

Curious to determine whether she found another secret room, Matilda strode over to the book and pushed it back into place. A quiet *snick* was audible as the book settled. She noticed the title, Shakespeare's *King Richard III*.

This was the second Shakespearean tome that was the entrance into the secret world she had found herself in. She pulled on the bookcase and noticed a hallway. She glanced back into her father's study and took notice of the time on the clock that sat on the mantle of the fireplace.

Matilda didn't have the time to explore as she wanted. So, she closed the door and proceeded to her rooms.

FROM THE DARKNESS of the secret hall, Percy thanked God that his inquisitive daughter hadn't decided to go exploring. Percy let out a sigh of relief. There was no way that he wanted Matilda to live in the shadows like he did. His life wasn't his own and hadn't been since he sold his soul to the devil—his wife's younger brother. There was no other name for the man. He was a double agent, and the risk of being caught was high.

As soon as the trap door snicked shut, he raced toward the hidden staircase and rushed up the stairs to his rooms. He didn't want to further Matilda's curiosity by showing up in his study—the room that she had just left.

Percy smiled despite himself. Matilda would have made a very good spy if he had allowed it, but his late wife's brother knew his wishes. Matilda could help decipher codes, but he would not allow her to go out in the field. He only hoped that his daughter wouldn't force his hand.

MATILDA STRODE INTO her rooms and laughed. She had found another secret passage to explore. She would have to thank the duke the next time she just happened to come across him—which would be sooner rather than later because of the carriage ride he promised her tomorrow.

She flopped down on her bed and laid there for a moment. An idea took root. Her father would leave and enter the house without anyone knowing the difference. He must have used the secret passageways. There was no other way he could do it without either her or the servants knowing about it.

Matilda smiled to herself. She needed to get into her father's rooms to see if there was a secret passage there, but would have to wait. Though, she kept thinking and thinking about her discovery. She was like a dog with a bone; she couldn't help but want to explore more. She really wanted to know where it led. As soon as she could, she would grab a candelabra and explore her new space. Maybe she could find another room, or maybe a spy's lair.

Matilda's imagination went wild. She could imagine a man sitting at a desk in a room that no one knew existed. He was planning his next mission. He would have maps of the area he was going to—in France?

With Napoleon in his prison on Elba, where would our spy go? she thought to herself. The war with the Americans ended a year ago. Waterloo ended the war with France months ago. There was India—in a pinch, but there was always someone causing problems in Scotland and Ireland. Even the lordlings on their tour caused a problem on the Continent.

It didn't matter anyway because the spy didn't truly exist. If she were to be honest with herself, she could see herself being that spy. Matilda shook her head. She knew that Uncle Anthony had made a promise to her mother that he would not train

Matilda in the art of intrigue.

For now, she would help Uncle Anthony decipher code and research—which was what she was supposed to be doing instead of daydreaming about a nameless, faceless spy.

SEVERAL HOURS LATER, Matilda heard her father's voice in the hall—telling the butler that he should not wait up for him. She knew that he would be out for the night, gambling more of their property away. She noticed her grandmother's silver disappearing. Same with the harp that used to stand regally next to her piano forte.

She picked up the stand of candles and made her way back to her father's study. She wanted to explore a bit before her father came back home. Matilda unlocked the secret door and opened it. She was surprised that there were no cobwebs, almost as if the hall had been polished like the ones in the main living areas. The hallway or passage should have been dustier.

Before long, Matilda came to a fork in the passage. To the right, she instinctively knew that would lead her back to some other room in her house. Straight ahead should take her to the mews. To the left should take her to the duke's townhouse?

She turned down the left corridor. She noticed a door much like the one in the study. She would need to find the mechanism to open the trap door.

IOAN WAS IN his study whining to himself about not going out when the strangest, most disturbing sound pulled him out of his thoughts.

If there was anything about the day that he would remember, it would be what happened after he heard something open—like a door. He reached into the top drawer of his desk, pulled the pistol out, and cocked the hammer—ready to fire.

As he turned toward the bookcase, he saw a little pixie woman stepping into his study. Ioan blinked, hoping that he was seeing an actual pixie and not Lady Matilda.

"Your Grace, it is a pleasure to see you!" The little pixie smiled.

Ioan couldn't believe his eyes, or his ears for that matter.

"Why is there a pixie in my study?" he whispered to himself—loud enough for the lady to hear.

Matilda giggled. "I am not a pixie, Your Grace. You see, I was just exploring this secret passage that I found earlier and decided that I would follow one corridor over the other…and here I am."

Here she was, in his study. In her night rail? Ioan threaded one hand through his hair. This could not be happening. She, Matilda, looked even more like a pixie than normal. The primal urge to kiss her was thrumming through his blood.

Ioan strode over to Matilda and took her hands in his. "You should not be here, my lady. You don't know me. I could take advantage of you, push you against the shelves, and take you. I might not be honorable."

"You are many things, Your Grace—dishonorable is not one of them," she whispered.

"You think so highly of me, my lady? I am going to kiss you. You have three seconds to tell me that you don't want me to."

Ioan waited. The pixie before him didn't move, her eyes wide. He slowly dipped his head down and brushed his lips against hers. Ioan pulled her closer, as if to draw Matilda into him. He groaned when she returned his kiss and melted into him. Good lord, she was a delight. He wanted more, but there was a mystery afoot.

Ioan pulled away from the passionate kiss. Apparently, Matilda enjoyed it just as much as he did—if the flush on her cheeks was any indication. He forced himself to take a step back.

"Your Grace, now that I know of this secret passage, I am

sure I can figure out how my father gets in and out of the house unnoticed. It has given me an idea of there being a passage leading up to his rooms—"

"You are not doing this alone, Matilda. I will not allow it," Ioan argued.

"You will not allow it? Oh, Your Grace, you have no right to dictate to me what I can or cannot do in my own house," Matilda shot back at him.

"Well then, little pixie, I am going with you." Ioan put his hands onto his hips. He watched as annoyance flashed in her eyes.

"If that's what you want. I am not little and I am—most definitely—not a pixie," Matilda said as she marched away from him.

Ioan couldn't believe what had just happened. Still in shock, he followed Matilda into the secret passage.

"MY FATHER'S ROOMS have a bookcase with old tomes. I haven't been in to see if there were any Shakespearean books—" Matilda strode down the hall to her father's rooms.

"What do you plan on doing once we get there?" Ioan asked.

"I have noticed some books that weren't securely placed in the bookcases in both the study and the music room. When I pushed them back, it unlocked a mechanism that opened the trap door," she recited back.

Matilda didn't stop walking and never stopped talking. She couldn't wait to see if there was a secret passage. Even more, that she could have more time with the duke.

She stepped up to the door leading into her father's apartment. She opened it, grabbed the duke's hand, and dragged him into the room.

Matilda leaned near him, pointed at the large bookcase opposite them, and whispered, "Do you see the book that's a little too far out?"

The duke nodded.

"That's how I can tell when there is a secret passage or room."

Without grabbing the duke's hand, she rushed over to the bookcase. Then she heard a loud *thwap* and something falling to the floor. She pivoted on her feet to see what happened. She noticed a man, her father, standing over the duke. "Father, what have you done?"

⎯⎯ · ⎯⎯ ◦❦◦ ⎯⎯ · ⎯⎯

Chapter Nine

IOAN'S HEAD HURT. He raised his hand and rubbed the part that hurt the most. He cringed. Somewhere in the background, he heard a man and a woman arguing. He recognized one of the voices—Matilda. The man with the same dark hair as Matilda must be her father?

"…you will have to marry him…" The man's voice echoed in his ears.

What? Marry Matilda? Though it wouldn't be much of a hardship, Ioan would have wanted to do things the right way—balls, carriage rides, courting. Not being forced to marry her at the insistence of her father—who had the right to insist they marry since they were caught in a bedroom together.

The only honorable way to go would be to marry the little pixie.

"I will marry her." He spoke quietly.

He couldn't quite believe he said it, but he felt right. He didn't believe in love at first sight, for god's sake, the woman ran into him and maimed him at their first encounter.

He glanced at Matilda, wishing his eyes would focus more. Her mouth hung open in shock—which, strangely enough, excited him. Why? Since the day they met, she was the one to shock him—she had knocked the breath out of him, quite literally. He had a theory that she composed her own music. She was a sleuth—she loved riddles and mysteries. Ioan couldn't have asked for a better woman to keep him on his toes.

"I will marry her," he said louder, in case the two hadn't heard him the first time.

"Glad to hear it," the older man replied. "Now, let me get arrangements made. The archbishop owes me a favor."

The archbishop? Well, the man could—at the very least— supply them with a special license to marry a bit more quickly. Ioan thought about his own contacts. His own godfather was a bishop in his own right—his father's younger brother.

Maybe this was a good thing after all.

"Why did you agree to marry me?" Matilda asked from where she stood several feet away.

"There are several different reasons, but I think that the one I like the most is the kiss we shared. It was beautiful; you are beautiful inside and out. Your love of music, of mysteries, of those you care about—calls to me. I won't say that I love you because I believe it is too soon for that. It feels right to me, little pixie. We feel right." Ioan strode up to Matilda, offering his hands up to her—and she took them in hers.

She nodded at him and Ioan rejoiced inside. They would make the best of the circumstances—he was sure. There was no way out, but he didn't want out.

"Let's go downstairs and await news from your father—the footman is throwing daggers at us through his eyes." Ioan notched his head toward the man guarding the door.

What he expected from Matilda wasn't what he heard. The woman giggled—and Ioan smiled.

MATILDA COULDN'T BELIEVE what she was hearing. A virtual stranger, someone she accidentally accosted outside of her home, was willing to marry her? She didn't know if she could trust the Scottish duke or not.

She supposed that he had been gentlemanly toward her since the ball. In his own way, he had told her he was interested in courting her. That kiss—though not her first—was the most memorable.

Matilda couldn't stop the flush cross her face. She noticed the duke staring at her. She bit her lower lip and blushed even more.

"What are you staring at?" she couldn't help but ask.

"The beautiful woman I will be marrying soon," the duke replied with a smile—a satisfied glint in his eyes.

She hadn't realized how long it had been since her father had left. *Why am I thinking about my father when I have a handsome man in front of me?*

"*Matilda!*" She heard her father bellow from the front hall.

Matilda knew that something wasn't right. There was pensiveness in her father's tone. She rushed to her feet and to her his side. He had a paper in his hands.

"The archbishop granted a special license. While I was in the room with the archbishop, another man entered stating that he knew His Grace and offered to do the deed for us—today."

Matilda gasped. In a few short hours, she would be married to the most eligible bachelor in the whole of England—and she was terrified. Well, not of the duke—but, of marriage? She was afraid of losing herself, of giving up what made her—well—her.

"When, Father?" she asked, wringing her hands.

"Now." Her father turned and allowed a gentleman into the hall.

"Good evening, my dear. Where is my rascal of a nephew?" the man asked as he bowed over her hand.

"He is right here, uncle."

Wait one moment, she said to herself. Matilda glanced between the two men. There couldn't have been more than a couple years between them and they looked almost identical. The only difference was the clothing they were wearing—the uncle in his robes of the church and the nephew in all his ducal finery.

She couldn't pull her eyes away from them.

"I think that we have made your intended bride speechless, Ioan." The uncle winked.

"Well, let's get this done with, shall we?" her father insisted.

The uncle nodded. "Matilda, my dear, do you agree to this match?" The bishop, for certainly he was acting more like the leader of the church rather than the fun-loving uncle he had been moments earlier.

Matilda couldn't help but nod.

"Very well."

In the hallway, the brief service, if one could call it that, occurred. Within a couple of moments, she was pronounced the new Duchess of Rathdrum and was pulled into the parlor to sign the registry and license.

Matilda's mind was adrift in a maelstrom of pure madness. There was no other explanation for the events that led to her impromptu wedding.

"Matilda?" The duke tried to gain her attention.

"Yes, Your Grace?" she replied.

The man snickered. "You may call me Ioan in private. Let's get you home."

⟫⟫⟩⟨⟨⟨

IOAN GLANCED OVER at his uncle. "I will see you tomorrow?"

The other man nodded his approval.

"I am going to get my wife settled."

To be honest, he had lost track of where Matilda was. She had snuck off somewhere—if the amazing sound coming from the music room was any indication, she needed to work through the recent events in her mind.

He motioned for his uncle to follow him.

"What am I hearing?"

"That would be the musical talent of my new wife." Ioan smiled as they came to the open door of the music room.

The piece that Matilda was performing was one that he had never heard played before. He had been proud of the fact that he was a connoisseur of the musical arts—and he still couldn't determine who the composer was.

He glanced over at his uncle who stood transfixed, listening to his pixie's genius.

"I have never—" his uncle started.

Ioan continued to watch as Matilda took his breath away with each sweeping movement. Until the music changed to something light and playful. He knew that she had worked out her problem and was content with her decision.

Once she closed the piano forte, Ioan clapped.

"That piece was beautiful. Who is the composer?" he asked from his place at the door.

"It was written by an obscure composer. You wouldn't know the person."

Ioan noticed her wringing her hands, as if waiting for confirmation of something. He knew in that instant that she had composed it herself. He couldn't be prouder of her. Working in a man's profession two times over—music composition and spy games.

Ioan smiled. "What is the name of the composer?"

"Robert Stroud," Matilda bashfully replied.

"Do you have any more of his work? I would like to try to sight read it, if I could."

Ioan couldn't have been more right. Matilda blushed at his words, and in his eyes, she couldn't be more beautiful.

"I have several of his pieces. Would you like to try them now?"

Ioan tried to hold back the riot of laughter but couldn't. "My little pixie, we must go to my townhouse. You can bring them with you." He tried to reassure Matilda, but was unsure that it made any affect at all.

Chapter Ten

MATILDA HAD STEPPED into world that she was unprepared for when she entered the ducal townhouse—on the arm of her handsome husband.

Since her mother's death, most of her training had been left to tutors and Uncle Anthony, since her father had been absent for most of her childhood. She was trained in some of the female arts but was woefully ignorant of others. She knew how to decipher code, she knew how to compose music, how to spend frivolous amounts on trivial things. She could tell when someone was lying to her, which was a gift and a curse. She also knew how to become friendly with the staff in her father's house.

Maybe, if Matilda used the same concept—she cut off her thoughts. She had to make the best of her situation; being Ioan's wife would not be a hardship.

"It is late, pixie," Ioan started. "Why don't I introduce you to the staff in the morning? That is, if you don't mind."

Matilda glanced into his eyes and saw the laughter in them. "I wouldn't want to wake the house this late." She looked for the godfather clock—much like the one in the hall of her father's house. After seeing the time, she agreed more with her thoughts of just going to bed.

"We don't have the duchess's rooms aired out, so you will be in my rooms today—tonight. If you don't feel comfortable with me in the bed, then I will sleep on the settee by the fireplace."

His words warmed her heart. He had acknowledged what her fear was and stopped it in its tracks. She was certain that he would expect his marital rights tonight. To know that he was giving her time had her melting inside.

"Thank you, Your Grace," she whispered bashfully.

Matilda followed her husband up the stairs to his rooms.

IOAN HAD A feeling that his pixie was having some anguish about the wedding night. He couldn't—wouldn't—ever force a woman to do anything she wasn't willing to do on her own. He would let her initiate their encounters. That didn't mean he was going to give up on keeping his hands to himself—brief touches, holding her hands, wrapping her in embraces, kissing—he just hoped that he could comfort her enough that she would soon enjoy the intimacy of being married.

Ioan pushed open the giant oak doors leading to his rooms. He hadn't changed anything from when his father was master of the house. The most imposing piece of furniture in the rooms was the massive medieval bed. It was truly ghastly. It had gargoyles carved into the large pillars on each of the four posts.

Until arriving at the townhouse, he had never seen a bed as big as the one in the ducal apartments.

He noticed a gasp come from Matilda's lips.

"I thought that beds such as this were only in gothic novels." She placed her hand on one of the pillars—and Ioan felt jealous.

"Unfortunately, I can't move the bed, but the mattress is constantly restuffed every couple of months with new feathers," he said, hoping to reassure her.

"Oh! I am not frightened. I find it most interesting." Matilda almost sounded breathless.

Ioan couldn't believe it. Even he was initially taken aback at the macabre scene that played out on the pillars.

"Well, I will let you prepare for bed. Would you like me to sleep on the settee?" he asked, watching for her response.

It came moments later in the form of a shake of her head and a barely audible, "No, that's not necessary. I trust you."

His little pixie humbled him. He hadn't always been a man to be trusted with the ladies. He had changed dramatically since the deaths of his family. He barely recognized himself.

"I am glad that you find the bed entertaining. I will be in my dressing room and will be out in a moment." Ioan hoped that this whole mess would look better in the morning.

The next morning was hectic. Introducing his new wife to the townhouse's—mostly Scottish—staff was a lesson in patience for Ioan. He knew that the men and women—his clansmen—held a great disdain for all things English. Ever since the Battle of Culloden and the dissolution of the clans.

Having an English bride was a contention among his loyal staff. Ioan prayed—which he didn't do very often—that Matilda would be able to charm them into loving her.

After leaving his pixie in the capable hands of his housekeeper—Mrs. Maddox—Ioan went to work in his office. Ioan had a business plan to go over with Finn and James, knowing they would want to—very possibly—work with him on it.

"*Your Grace!*" Mrs. Maddox stormed into his study.

Calmly, Ioan asked, "What can I do for you, Mrs. Maddox?"

"You must come to the music room. Her Grace is causing quite the scene!"

Ioan guffawed at his irate housekeeper. "She is playing the piano forte, is she?"

"Yes, Your Grace, and the maids and footmen are distracted. They won't work!" The woman put her hands on her hips and stared into his eyes.

"My dear Mrs. Maddox, my lovely bride has the gift of music, and if she wants to play for our staff, then let them enjoy her talent. It has been way too long since music has been played in this house."

Mrs. Maddox glared at him before storming back out of the room.

Ioan held back the laughter, pulled himself up from the chair, and strode toward the music room—hearing what was bewitching his staff. He recognized the reel that she was playing, a Scottish tune written by some long ago person who the world no longer knew.

He noticed that some of the staff were dancing in the room, since it was big enough for multiple couples to dance. Though, when one of the footmen noticed him, they stopped. The dancers scurried to go back to work.

Ioan strolled toward his bride, put his arms around her, and kissed the top of her head.

"Am I in trouble?" she asked.

"No, but you may have made an enemy of our housekeeper," Ioan replied with a grin.

"Oh! I don't want that. I must work with her. How do I get back into her good graces?"

"You will find a way, I'm sure of it. I would suggest learning the Old Scots song called 'The Earl of Brackley,'" he said as he winked at her.

He surveyed her lovely face, taking in the smile that made her glow. He knew that the housekeeper wouldn't be able to withstand singing if Matilda started playing the song. Ioan dropped another kiss to the top of her head before leaving the room.

⇶⫷

MATILDA WAS SHOCKED. Flabbergasted. In awe of what had happened. She would need to ask Ioan for the sheet music or have a Scottish music master to instruct her on how to play for the ill-tempered housekeeper.

She couldn't forget having her husband's arm around her. He

was affectionate. If she were to be honest, she enjoyed it. Matilda loved being the center of someone's affection—which she had never had before. Even from her uncle, who was more like a rowdy older brother to her.

She smiled. She put her fingers on the keyboard and continued to play.

What seemed like hours later, Matilda stepped into her husband's study. The room smelled of leather, polish, and Ioan. The room was very masculine—just as she remembered.

Matilda crossed over to where Ioan was bent over his desk—reading and writing on something.

"What are you working on?" She sidled toward him.

"A business venture. Your uncle seems to be too busy for domestic investigations. I thought I would start an arm of his operations," Ioan replied.

Interested in what he was doing, Matilda walked around the desk and took a seat in one of the chairs opposite him. "You need manpower; have you figured out who you would hire?"

Ioan smiled. "Of course, we would hire displaced military. Those who can't find work. We would deal mostly with high-end crimes; murder, theft, kidnapping, and the like. Espionage and treason would be for your uncle to deal with."

"What about capital? I know that a couple of your friends are mixed in with Uncle Anthony's business." Matilda sank back in her chair, getting comfortable.

"We could use your intellect. Your way with code and your memory, I hear, is almost as good as mine."

Matilda leaned forward. "Do you want to test me?"

"Maybe later. Your memory when it comes to music is second to none. You don't have to prove yourself to me." Ioan smiled at her.

It was true. Matilda was accomplished at the piano forte and had memorized all her pieces after playing them once. She didn't have to have a cypher to decode the messages her uncle sent her because she had them memorized. Every book, phrase, and word that she had read throughout the years were engrained in her mind—ready to be brought forth at any time to discuss or to be used for code.

It was to, finally, get the recognition that she had been craving her whole life. That wasn't saying that Uncle Anthony didn't recognize her abilities—he certainly did—but she wanted to be known for something outside of the spy community.

Matilda wanted more, and she knew, that with Ioan by her side, she would be able to find what she was meant to be all along.

Chapter Eleven

MATILDA, WEARING A gorgeous periwinkle gown with an over-gown of Irish lace, sat in her new parlor. Ioan had made sure that hothouse flower arrangements decorated the room for her. She was picking through some of Ioan's books from the library just across the hall.

She happened to glance up just as a footman entered.

"Your Grace, you have a visitor. A Lady Dearling?"

Matilda jumped to her feet. Elizabeth Dearling was the first friend she ever had. "Yes, please send her in," she said excitedly.

Elizabeth ran, if you could call it running, into the room, engulfing her in her arms. "Why didn't you write to me to tell me you were married?" Beth *hmphed*.

"It was just a couple of days ago. Do you remember how busy you were when you took over the Rosewood Estate?" Matilda remembered the day as if it was yesterday.

Matilda had been at the wedding of Elizabeth and her very dear husband, Andrew Parkington—the Earl of Rosemont.

Matilda remembered that. Even though her friend had not gone on a wedding trip, she had been busy for weeks after due to taking over the household accounts. Or that's what Beth had said.

"I recall that very well, indeed." Beth grinned.

"That's not what I meant and you know it." Matilda blushed as she tapped her friend on her shoulder.

"I couldn't help myself. Making you blush is so easy to do."

"There is something I would like to bring to your attention, if I may?" Matilda asked, trying to change the subject of the conversation.

"By all means." Beth cocked her head.

"My husband is wanting to start a new investigative branch of Tarleton's department at Whitehall…"

"I heard about that from Andrew. You know I've been helping Rathdrum with his speculative prospects for years—well, it wouldn't be such a stretch to help with the finances for this new venture."

Matilda loved her friend and enjoyed the intellectual discussions. Where Matilda's mind remembered everything she read, Elizabeth had a mind for numbers.

"I think that Ioan could use your expertise. I would like for you to speak with him, if you wouldn't mind."

"Of course. I would love to speak with him about this," Beth said.

Matilda smiled. "If he asked me to help him with this venture, I don't think that he would have a problem listening to your thoughts. In fact, he is waiting for you now. I will lead you to his study." She grabbed hold of Beth's arm and nearly dragged her to Ioan's study.

IOAN SAT BEHIND his desk, hands steepled together, listening to Finn and James harass their other friend, Andrew. All four of them had grown up together, including their formative years, at Eton. They had gotten into a lot of trouble over the years until war broke out on the Continent. The boys had been at an age to read about the exploits of Admiral Nelson, but not nearly old enough to take up arms and buy commissions. James and Finn entered the war efforts as soon as they were out of university. Ioan and Andrew had family issues that caused them to seek other ways to pitch in.

Ioan leaned back in his chair and smiled when he noticed Matilda dragging her friend into the study.

James, Finn, and Andrew glanced up at the same time and Ioan threw his head back with laughter.

"Let me introduce you to Pixie…um…Matilda, and you all remember Elizabeth, Andrew's wife," Ioan introduced as Matilda strode to him and he pulled her into his side.

"A little bird told me that you are starting a new venture—" Elizabeth started the conversation.

"We are. An investigation arm of Whitehall. We would, alongside Lord Tarleton, handle the domestic crimes." Ioan pushed a pile of vellum sheets toward Elizabeth.

Ioan watched with fascination when Elizabeth read through his ideas—his proposal to Tarleton.

"It seems that you have thought of everything, Your Grace," Elizabeth stated.

"Yes. The funding of the project is in there too. We can't expect funding from Whitehall. We can supplement with our own purses, but we can only support it so much before our estates suffer."

Ioan knew what a risk a venture like this would be. He needed to find other ways to get money.

"You know that Whitehall has an allotted amount of funds to help in a venture such as this. Talk with Lord Tarleton. He is on the committee for that department." She smiled.

"I told you my wife would know what to do," Andrew said gaily.

Ioan had known that Elizabeth was smart when it came to numbers. He had gone to Rosemont Park before, much before he became duke for advice on increasing his investments. With Elizabeth's help, he was able to live comfortably off his own money and invested his quarterly allowance in ventures and the money markets.

"You know that's what I would have advised. Why have me

look at this?" she asked.

Ioan contemplated his thoughts before replying. "I wanted to see or hear your advice. I would also like to extend an invitation for you to join our little enterprise." Ioan glanced into his friend's wife's eyes. He saw the glint of tears forming in them.

"I don't know what to say," Elizabeth replied, sniffling.

Ioan smiled. He knew that his invitation was unheard of for women, yet he was never a man who did anything by society's standards. "Welcome to our venture, Lady Dearling."

PERCY THANKED GOD for the first time in his life. His daughter was safe and in the arms of a wealthy duke, even if the man was Scottish. His enemies no longer had that hold over him. He had overlooked letting Tarleton know about Matilda's marriage. That problem would need to be dealt with post haste.

Percy checked the clock. It was still early. He could reach Tarleton's offices before the man left for the night. Instead of walking, like he would normally do, he would have to ride. He called for a footman to have the stable lads saddle a horse for him.

Thirty minutes later, Percy stood outside of Tarleton's office preparing himself for the conversation he was about to have. He slowly raised his hand to knock on the door when a voice from inside told him to enter.

"What brings you here, Percy?" Tarleton asked.

"Your niece has married the Duke of Rathdrum," Percy replied.

"I know. Matilda managed to send me a missive the day after the nuptials. My question to you is, why did it take so long for you to come to me with the happy news?"

Percy struggled with his words. He hadn't considered that his daughter had the presence of mind to write a missive after her nuptials

"How was I supposed to know?" he asked.

"You should know your daughter. I think, over the years, I have done you a great disservice. I have been the one to raise Matilda while you were off doing my bidding. It was my fault. You needed a purpose. You felt like my sister's death was the child's fault. Now, I know her better than you and she comes to me when things go awry," Tarleton exclaimed.

Percy knew that his brother by marriage, and his handler, spoke the truth. There was nothing he could say that would alter that.

"I thought I would have a couple of days to get to you about this. Unfortunately, that wasn't the case," Percy replied.

It never occurred to him that he was not in his boss's good graces. Not at all. Tarleton wasn't someone to anger because his bark, by far, was worse than his bite.

"I am sorry, my lord." Percy tried to appeal to the man's good sense of empathy when it came to Matilda. "It won't happen again."

"Of course it won't happen again. You only have the one daughter. Unless you have another child that I am unaware of—"

Percy bit his lip. He hadn't been a monk since his wife died in childbirth. He had seduced many a woman to get information over the years. He knew of, at least, one other child that he had sired.

"For God's sake, Percival! How many?" Tarleton bellowed as the man rounded his desk toward Percy.

"One, that I am aware of." Percy ran his fingers through his already disheveled hair.

He watched as Tarleton tried to keep his anger under control. It wasn't anything that Percy hadn't thought about himself. He was the worst, most vile man he knew. He would do whatever it took for the Crown—including, occasionally having sex with those he wanted to gain information from. Percy had no qualms with showing his affection with either sex. In fact, he enjoyed an occasional menage. He knew his preferences were unusual, but to him, it was well worth it.

"One? Are you sure?" Tarleton pushed Percy into the wall.

"Yes, just one. I pay for the child's upkeep, quarterly. I know I've gone against our code, but I wouldn't have gotten the information necessary to put Napoleon in his island prison without it. We would still be fighting that bastard if I hadn't," Percy argued.

Tarleton glance at him, murder in his eyes. "Never again. Do you hear me? Never again—or by the deity, I will end you—regardless of how your daughter feels about it. Do I make myself clear?"

AFTER PERCY LEFT his office, Tarleton smiled at his ingenious plan. Matilda would thank him in the long run. Now, to do some more digging into the deaths of two of his best agents. He had an idea of who it might be, but he would have to investigate more.

Anthony thought of Matilda's request for more cases. Somewhere deep inside, he knew that her marriage to the Duke of Rathdrum was fortuitous. He needed the help with solving these cases on British soil. The duke would be a great asset, much like his father and brothers before him.

He would send a missive to the man at his earliest convenience and hope that Rathdrum would agree to his terms.

Anthony steepled his fingers under his chin. *Maybe, an in-person conversation would be better for this,* he thought to himself. He would ride to Matilda's new house and surprise them with a visit.

Chapter Twelve

MATILDA WAS SHOCKED to see her uncle outside her door. Obviously, since she was at home and her uncle was outside, neither of them had any social plans for the evening—outside of having the venture members over for a meeting.

Matilda allowed a footman to do his job by opening the door—then she raced in to embrace her uncle.

"Uncle Anthony, what are you doing here?"

"I heard from a little bird that there has been talk of an investigative arm of my department."

At that moment, Ioan strolled up to her and wrapped his arms around her waist, showing off his protective—or was it possessive?—nature.

"What can we help you with, Tarleton?" Ioan asked.

"If you don't mind, can I speak with you about your new venture? I hate to admit it, but I need help. I have a case, your case, that I need help with. Do you need employees, or do you need any resources to get you started?"

Matilda stared at her uncle. She thought that it would have been more of a fight with her uncle to see how much this enterprise could help Uncle Anthony's department and missions. Apparently, she didn't know her uncle as well as she thought she did.

"We were just speaking about coming to visit you about this." Ioan smiled. "In fact, we were just holding a meeting ourselves."

Matilda couldn't help but smile to herself. She turned toward the study and motioned for Uncle Anthony to follow her. When she got to the room, the men rose from their chairs and watched as Matilda summoned Tarleton to enter with her.

"I see that two of my men are already in on your new venture, Rathdrum," Tarleton exclaimed after shaking the hands of the men in the room.

Matilda knew that having her uncle join the meeting was a good idea, but she felt an unease creep through her. She felt arms snake around her middle again and leaned back into her husband's arms.

"I know that something isn't right. I can feel it too." Ioan brushed his lips across her cheek.

Matilda shivered at the small sparks that lit her body as Ioan's breath continued to waft across her skin.

"Rathdrum, do you have a proposal for your new enterprise?" Tarleton asked.

Matilda felt her husband's arms pull away from her as Ioan crossed the room to his desk, pulled the large packet from a drawer, and handed it to the other man.

Moments later, arms stole around her once more. It surprised her how much comfort she felt with him nearby. They had barely known each other a month and she couldn't imagine a world without him in it. He was protective of her, he made her feel safe, he was intellectual, and he was a conversationalist that kept her on her toes. There was more that she liked about him, but she didn't have time to dwell on those things now. Her safety and comfort was paramount to anything else, at least, that's what her story was—and she was sticking to it.

She knew that time would either cure her of that feeling or make it stronger. She hoped—and dare she say, prayed—that it would be the latter and not the former.

She didn't register the conversation going on. All she could think about were the arms banded around her, the broad chest that was behind her, and the steady stream of breaths causing sparks to skitter up and down her spine.

"...Matilda, what do you think?" Her uncle's voice finally broke through her musings.

"I think that the venture could help you and the Crown. Leaving the domestic operations to these men would, in fact, lighten your cases and give you more time with your agents." She sounded as if she had rehearsed that—which she had.

Uncle Anthony nodded. "Who do you plan to hire?"

Matilda waited a moment to allow anyone else to reply. When no one else said a word, she blurted out, "Former militia. Those who came back injured or are in need of work. The honorable and those who fought with distinction and valor."

"I like that," her uncle exclaimed. "It is an honorable thing you are willing to do. There are many men who came home from Waterloo to find out that there weren't any jobs available to them. I know of some men who you might want to visit with."

Matilda glanced over at her uncle as he handed a sheet of vellum to James. She peeked over at the man and watched as, what looked like joy, came over his face.

"These men were all part of my company." James shot to his feet, causing Matilda to jump.

She felt Ioan's arms enclose around her shoulders.

"I know you were worried about them. Since they are gentry, they can be invited to social events that some of your other men won't be able to get into. I would suggest hiring them first. I will pay the wages through my department, and any travel expenses. Lady Dearling, if you would please do the accounting for me, I would be forever in your debt." Tarleton bowed and exited the room.

Ioan pulled Matilda in closer to him. He loved the feel of her in his arms, safe and sound. He had never been the kind of man that was possessive with his lovers, but having a wife certainly brought out that trait in him.

Ioan tucked Matilda's head under his chin and held tight.

"Well, it looks like we need to get my men and take a wee trip to Scotland." James didn't seem happy about going back to the Highlands. Ioan would have to ask him about that later.

"James, do you still have that ship at the ready?" Finn asked.

"Of course I do. I wish that I didn't have to go back up there so soon after my previous trip." James shot Ioan a menacing glare.

Ioan couldn't hold back the laughter bubbling up inside him. "I do apologize, James, but I need to get to my family records. I don't believe I can solve this case without them."

"My sister, Gloria, will want me to run her to the shops if she finds out I'm there," the man whined.

"I can't stop my staff from gossiping. You will just have to spend a day with Gloria. Maybe Matilda would like to join you." Ioan glanced down at her and winked.

He smiled as her face brightened to a deep red. She was so innocent. They had not yet consummated the marriage and he enjoyed that he could arouse her emotions. He could probably arouse other things as well, but he had promised Matilda that any intimacies would be at her pace—except for kissing and touching.

Ioan had to step back from the hold he had on Matilda. His cock wanted inside her. He wanted her more with each passing moment. He couldn't rush her. She was barely able to stand his need to touch her, hold her, or embrace her. Her uncle and father had damaged the poor girl. Ioan had his work cut out for him.

TARLETON STEPPED INTO his carriage and told the driver to go to his townhouse. Unlike the townhouses by the duke's, his was in an older part of town that the *Ton* no longer found fashionable. If he were honest with himself, he preferred to have his small house that only his driver knew about.

Anthony smiled to himself. His plan—well, more like his niece's plan—was coming to fruition. He would have access to the Rathdrum libraries. He had a missing heir to a dukedom to find somewhere near Waterloo.

Chapter Thirteen

IOAN HELPED MATILDA board the *Nautilus*, James' passenger ship. He was not looking forward to the journey north, especially this time of year. Even in the port at Plymouth, the boat was rocking to and fro. He thanked God that he never joined the navy—because of the never-ending seasickness that he had each time he stepped foot onto a boat or ship. By the looks of it, his beautiful wife didn't have the same affliction as he did.

Ioan climbed aboard and helped Matilda to the cabin that would be theirs for the duration of the trip. The cabin had been the one that he had when he had come to England. It was cozy. The ship had been made to ferry people and had been built for luxury. He didn't understand how it could have any luxuries. There were no beds, and the cook made the same meals every day—and the passengers ate what the crew ate. Still, the hammocks tied to the walls were of the finest quality—or that was what he was told by James.

"This ship is so beautiful James owns it?" Matilda asked.

"He does; he is part owner of the shipping company. This is his personal ship that he takes to do his government work." Ioan placed the hat he had been wearing on the small chest of drawers that stood between the two hammocks.

"It was nice of him to loan us the use of such a majestic ship," Matilda commented.

Ioan's lips curved into a grin. It was, indeed, nice of his friend.

Though James would be going with them, rather than riding to Scotland.

"It was in his best interest, my dear. He, of course, is coming with us. It would be in his favor to transport all of us to Edinburgh. Now, let's get our things put away and meet with the others in the captain's cabin." Ioan had the overwhelming desire to kiss her.

He stepped closer to Matilda and held out his arms. When she stepped into his open embrace, he rejoiced. He held her to him, enjoying the feel of her body near his. He reached his hands to cup her face, bent down, and brushed his lips against hers. He pulled her closer and closer until there wasn't any space between them. He reveled in the feeling. Matilda started to kiss him back, so he deepened the kiss.

As Ioan's hands slid toward Matilda's breast, a loud knock on the door forced them apart. Ioan quickly righted himself, motioned for Matilda to stand behind him, and then opened the door to find Finn standing outside the door—his arms perched on his hips.

"Our beloved captain would like our presence on deck." Finn chuckled. "Oh and, Your Grace, you may want to straighten up a bit more before coming topside."

Ioan growled. Wait a moment, growled? He shook himself. He never growled. Ioan heard a gasp behind him as Matilda struggled to hold back laughter. Ioan closed the door and pivoted on his feet to face his beautiful wife, who still held a hand in front of her face to stifle her laughter.

He pulled her toward him and delighted in a short shriek. "We should probably get put together before heading up to the captain's cabin. James doesn't like being kept waiting—even for a duke and duchess."

MANY MILES AWAY, Tarleton stood on the deck of his own ship waiting for his no-good brother by marriage to arrive before sailing for the Continent.

Percy had the deciphered code that Anthony needed to find a lost lordling, and he was the only person he trusted to do it.

The duke of Blackthorn was dying from old age, and the only heir to the dukedom was injured during the Battle of Waterloo and had gone missing once the dust—or mud in this instance—settled. The child, now nineteen, had been missing for months.

Anthony hoped that the young man was holed up some-where with someone taking care of his wounds. Anthony would much prefer the best case scenario rather than the worst. He knew that he would be having nightmares. He always did while on a rescue mission.

"Who are we going to find this time?" Percy asked.

"Edward Harris, the apparent heir of the Duke of Black-thorn."

"I remember that young man. I was close to his father before the accident. Rumor was the father bought the boy a commission not realizing that he was heir of his maternal grandfather's title and estate."

If there was anything Anthony liked about Percy, it was the man's ability to remember details. Between Percy's gift and his sister's intelligence, his niece had both of those gifts. Somewhere in the back of his mind, Anthony knew that Matilda would choose to work with her husband rather than with him.

He could deal with the loss, but he needed someone to take her place. Luckily, the young man he was trying to find had the same unique gifts that Matilda and the Duke of Rathdrum had.

"When are we off?" Percy asked.

Anthony had to laugh. It would escape Percy's mind that they were already on the move. The giant sheets of canvas unfurled and caught the wind. The sounds of sailors going about their duties and the waves crashed into the hull.

IN THE DARKNESS of night, Mr. Black stood in the mews behind Lord Tarleton's house. He knew that the spy master was gone. He witnessed the man climb into his carriage. The man had packed for an extended stay.

Mr. Black couldn't get over his good luck. The servants were already asleep, which made his job of sneaking into Tarleton's office much easier. He instinctively knew that the doors would be locked tight, since the lord of the house was not in residence. The windows would be locked, as well—except, Mr. Black knew ways of breaking in through windows that not many knew of.

He rummaged around in the bag that he brought with him for his tools. Once he found what he needed, he strode up to the house—light-footed—and proceeded to jimmy open the window enough to allow him entry.

Mr. Black was not a big man. Standing at barely five foot, five inches and weighing as much as an adolescent boy, he was able to get into places that most men wouldn't be able to.

Once inside, on sure feet, Mr. Black crept up the stairs to Tarleton's office. The decryption code should be here. If not, it would be at the man's Whitehall office—and that would be nearly impossible to get into.

Mr. Black entered the office. The room was surprisingly clean. The desk was devoid of any papers, no clutter—at all. The bookshelves were immaculately put together. Not a single book was out of place. The organization was perfect. Each book was placed by author—alphabetically, and then by title—alphabetically.

Mr. Black was shocked. Never had he seen an office or study so—he had no words whatsoever. He moved to the desk and opened it—nothing. What the? There were nothing in any of the drawers. No ink or sheets of foolscap or quills. No paintings. Nothing. He was duped by the master himself. He wished that he could slap himself.

There was nothing for it. He would have to try to get into Whitehall. Otherwise, Tarleton had a house elsewhere that he knew nothing about.

Mr. Black turned toward the door. His brain didn't register what was in front of him until something hit him and everything went black.

"...GO GET MASTER Elijah," a man's voice broke through the pain in his head.

Who was Master Elijah? Where in the hell was he? He briefly remember Tarleton's office and then a furious pain in his head before waking up in whatever room he was in.

A tall, slender gentleman strode into the room. The man was dressed in black and white, reeking of money. The kind of gentleman that Mr. Black hated beyond belief.

"So, you are finally awake. My dear friend would be pleased," the man said. "Let me take a look at your head."

Mr. Black lashed out at the man named Elijah. The man raised his arms in a sign of surrender. "I am a doctor, man. I had my schooling at the Edinburgh school of medicine and I promise not to hurt you further. You know our oaths." The man strode back over to the bed.

Mr. Black conceded. His head hurt like a—he cut off his thoughts as Elijah touched his scalp.

"Bloody hell!" Black screamed as Elijah probed the spot on the top of his head where he was hit.

"Calm down, sir. Now, let me see your eyes." The other man tilted Black's head up to meet his eyes.

The light of the candle hurt. He closed them as soon as he could.

"You might be concussed. You will need to stay here for a

couple of days," the doctor said.

Black cringed. He was supposed to report back to his master in two days—with the decryption code. *Damn and blast it all to hell and back!* He could get in trouble—there was no could, he *would* get in trouble for this. It may be the end of him.

"Doctor Elijah, I need to leave now," Black bellowed from the bed.

"As you can see, sir, you cannot move. You have been restrained. We don't like robbers at this residence. You will not be leaving until I tell you that you can. That very well may be until Tarleton comes back." The man pivoted and strode out of the room.

Black would have to deal with the consequences of being caught. Or he could admit defeat and show the doctor who he really was—and hopefully, get some asylum. For the first time, in his life, Black felt at peace and fell asleep.

Chapter Fourteen

MATILDA WATCHED THE duke's massive house come into view. She had seen her share of manor houses, but this one seemed so much larger. It must be the mountains in the background or the sweeping valley in the foreground.

Between their carriage and the manor house, a ruined castle lay amidst a cluster of trees. Though ruined, it made an impressive sight. The beauty of it comforted her in the same way music did.

"That is our clan's old residence. When the new house was built, the castle fell into ruin," Ioan whispered into her ear.

Matilda felt sparks and shivers race through her. She was on the edge of something exciting and scary. She didn't understand the nuances of what she was feeling emotionally or physically.

Matilda burrowed into Ioan's side, enjoying the warmth of his presence. She couldn't help but feel calm and secure—like no one could ever hurt her while being in his arms. She could feel a kiss placed on her hair at the top of her head.

Before long, the carriage came to a halt in front of the house's giant wood doors. A line of servants who Ioan called "staff" waited for them to exit the carriage. Matilda hoped that they would slowly accept her like the staff in London had.

Matilda was nervous as she strode with Ioan up to the staff. A small rock caused her to stumble. Yet again, she stumbled into Ioan and accidentally elbowed him in the stomach. She watched as Ioan moaned in pain. "Are you well?"

Ioan's look of pain mixed with concern had her laughing. Laughing was her defense against anything painful.

"I think my pride will be fine as soon as my stomach stops hurting," Ioan said as he stood straighter.

Matilda glanced at the staff waiting for them. Each of the men and women looked as if they were going to a brawl—ready to attack at any moment.

"Lass, you may want to grab my arm," Ioan advised as he reached out to her.

Matilda noticed the Scottish brogue breaking through in his speech. She grabbed hold of her husband's arm and walked up to the men and women, who moments earlier looked like they were going to murder her where she stood.

"Ladies and gentlemen, I would like to introduce you to my wife, Matilda. Please, help her to get to know you and the house." With that, Ioan guided her down the line, introducing her to every single one of the household staff.

Matilda was then led into the house to the ducal apartments. She had seen a few luxurious houses, but these were beyond anything she had seen before.

"These are my rooms. You can share them with me, or you can have the duchess's rooms, which are directly through that door." Ioan pointed at a mural wall.

Matilda thought for a moment, weighing her options. She had been sharing a room with Ioan since their marriage ceremony. She would miss his presence. Even though they hadn't slept in the same bed, at least, not yet.

"I would rather be with you," she said shyly.

"Brave, my little pixie," her husband replied.

"I would hate for you to sleep in that rather uncomfortable chaise lounge," she teased him.

"Are you ready for that, pixie? If you aren't, I am going to make a cozy place by the fire to sleep."

Matilda knew her face flushed the brightest of red, which

made her flush even more. She twisted her hands in her skirts, trying to tame her body, but it didn't work. She reached out to touch Ioan. She felt compelled to.

She placed her hand on his face and felt the warmth of his skin permeate her being. Over the last couple weeks, she had craved touch, as if she was starved. At first, Ioan's need to continually touch her was maddening. She didn't want it. She, quite literally, burned at his contact with her skin. It hurt her beyond all belief.

Now, it still hurt, but she had become used to it. The pain subsided into something else; she didn't know what. She glanced up to Ioan's eyes and noticed something. She didn't know what it meant, but she could guess—need, lust, want.

Matilda stepped closer, seeking him and getting into his space. She needed to feel his arms around her; she felt overwhelmed by the feelings that swamped her. She didn't know how to ask for what she needed. Matilda hoped that Ioan could glean from her eyes, or even her actions, what that need was.

IOAN COULD TELL that Matilda was in distress. He slowly wrapped his arms around her and pulled her close. He waited for her to rest her head on his chest. Ioan held her there for some time, soaking in the feeling of her giving into what he could offer her— comfort.

Ioan relaxed. He could only guess at what she wanted and, apparently, this time, he was correct. "Love," he tilted her chin up to stare into her eyes. "Is something wrong?"

Matilda's eyes glittered with unshed tears. "Nothing is wrong. I just needed this, you. I won't be using the duchess's rooms. I want you."

Ioan was surprised. Matilda's eyes were still on him, hopeful. He couldn't deny her. If she wanted him, she would have him.

He tipped her chin up further.

"May I kiss you, my wee pixie? May I show you the pleasure you can find in my arms?" Ioan waited for a response. He felt the barest of movements against his chest. "My darling, no one is going to need us at this moment. Let's rest from our journey." Ioan wiggled his eyebrows and delighted in the giggles he heard as he picked her up and hurried to his bed.

Ioan playfully tossed Matilda and watched as she sank into the feather bed. He climbed in next to her, pulling her closer to him. "My pixie," he whispered in her ear. He smiled when he felt her shiver. He tilted her head up and brushed his lips against hers. The kiss was an introduction, a prelude of what would come next.

Ioan coaxed Matilda's mouth open enough to plunge his tongue into the warm cavern and stroke his tongue against hers while deepening the kiss. God Almighty! He could barely think. All the blood in his head rushed down to his hardening manhood.

He let his hands start to wander, still feeling the fabric of the walking gown that she had been wearing since they departed the ship. The scent of salt water still clung to her skin and the fabric of the gown.

Ioan berated himself for not undressing her—or himself, for that matter—before they reached the bed. It was an oversite that he would have to remedy poste haste. He climbed out of the bed and pulled Matilda with him.

If there was anything Ioan couldn't do while thoroughly aroused, it was take the time to completely disrobe before making love. He was used to the women who would pull up their skirts and rut with men anytime or anywhere. But, he couldn't do that with his wife—at least, not the first time. Images flew through his mind of taking her against the wall, in the pond, in the field, against a tree—God, he had it bad.

He needed her to be drunk with pleasure. He needed her to be addicted to what he could make her feel so that she would need him inside her—often. Even through the fog that encompassed his mind, he knew that every pass of his hand on her skin would inch her ever higher, toward her climax.

Ioan undid the clasp that held the neckline of her gown together, then took the pins out of her hair, carefully pacing them on a small table next to the bed. He pulled the gown down and let it pool at her feet. Ioan couldn't have imagined how beautiful his pixie was under her gown.

Ioan pulled on the strings that kept her stays together. As they gradually loosened the garment, he brushed his fingers over the skin that was exposed.

MATILDA FELT OVERWHELMED by the feelings that Ioan stirred within her. She couldn't help but lean her head down against his muscled chest. She was expecting fingers to roam her exposed neck. She felt something altogether different, his lips.

The sound coming from her lips was strange to her ears as another moan escaped when Ioan's lips ran over every inch of her neck.

"Please—" Matilda heard herself plead.

Her shift and stays fell to the floor. She stepped over the garments and into her husband's waiting arms.

Chapter Fifteen

The joy blossoming in his chest spread through every part of his body. He couldn't believe his luck. To have his pixie in his arms, rejoicing in his touch, vocalizing her pleasure. God, he wanted more—so much more.

Matilda's voice beckoned his thoughts back to the present. "Your Grace, you are significantly overdressed." The twinkle in her eyes had him rushing to pull off his clothing as quickly as he could.

This playful side of his wife had escaped his notice. Ioan winked at her as he swiftly pulled his shirt over his head and heard Matilda gasp. He knew he could look imposing. He was tall and muscular—and in his prime.

"I won't hurt you, darling," he spoke in a deep, dark tone. He stalked toward her slowly.

It surprised him when she held out her arms and beckoned him to her. Instead of going into her arms, he picked her up and carried her to the bed. He gloried in the weight of her, her beautiful body against his, and that of her beautiful presence.

He put her on the bed, her hips sitting on the edge, his body cradled in the space between her thighs. Matilda's legs wrapped around him as he bent his head to meet her lips in a frenzied kiss, both bruising and passionate.

Ioan couldn't hold back. One hand ran down her body, taking in every curve, dip, and texture. He couldn't get enough. "Get into the middle of the bed," Ioan growled.

He stood still, watching as Matilda shimmied toward the middle of the bed and laid flat on her back. Her head turned toward him and Ioan saw every bit of emotion in her beautiful eyes. He saw wonder, excitement, arousal, need, and dare he say—love? He knew it was too soon for the latter, but he could only hope that one day, maybe, love may come into the picture.

"There is nothing to be afraid of, my beautiful pixie." Ioan climbed up next to her and swiftly kissed down her elegant neck and to her breasts.

Ioan had never seen such succulent breasts. The nipples were a rosy hue and perfect. He pulled one of the perfect peaks into his mouth and feasted on its perfection—alternating between nibbling on it and sucking.

The sounds coming from Matilda urged him on. He slowly kissed a path to the other rosy peak and laved it, loved it, and teased it. In the background, Ioan could hear Matilda moan and cry his name, signaling her need for him.

He couldn't hold back. "My darling pixie, open your legs wide for me." Ioan groaned, barely holding back his impending orgasm.

MATILDA DIDN'T UNDERSTAND what was happening to her; all she knew was she felt like she was going to combust—spontaneously. Every touch, every kiss made her ache for something that she had never experienced before.

"I...want..." She didn't know the words, but she needed to end the delicious torture that Ioan was putting her through.

"I will give you what you need, pixie," Ioan whispered in her ear.

Matilda felt one of Ioan's hands move down to her most intimate places—and stroke the little nub there. Something coiled deep inside her, threatening to release at any moment.

"Not yet, pixie." Ioan slowed his torture.

In that moment, he plunged a finger deep inside her, thrusting in and out. *Oh God! She needed*—her thoughts broke apart and scattered into little fragments as the release took her by surprise.

She felt Ioan move between her legs, his manhood nestled near her opening. She needed him, and that's all she could make sense of as she waited for him to take her.

"Look at me, pixie," Ioan whispered.

She glanced up at him with barely opened eyes.

"You can stop me now. If you don't, I am going to make you mine in every way. Do you want me to stop?"

All Matilda could do was nod and mouth the words "no, don't stop." In that moment, she couldn't believe what she was about ready to do. Ioan brought his face down to hers in a gloriously passionate duel of lips, teeth, and tongues. She felt him move on her as his member breached her feminine folds. She did the one thing she could do—and that was gasp.

"This may hurt a little, but I will make the rest pleasurable." Ioan took her mouth again in a bruising kiss as his cock nudged against her maidenhead. Matilda couldn't help squirming—trying to get away from the pressure building inside her.

Then with no warning, Ioan thrust deep—and she cried out at the searing pain. Ioan kissed her again and she let herself calm down, the pressure and pain slowly ebbing. Then she felt Ioan move in and out of her in even, sure strokes. A blossom of pleasure peeked through the receding pain. Matilda gasped again.

IOAN GROANED, AS he thrust into her hot, tight sheath. He felt her inner muscles clutch at him—trying to milk him of every ounce of his essence. He felt his own body race toward release, his need driving him to heights he had never achieved with any other woman.

"Come, love. Come!" he shouted as his climax struck him. Somewhere in the back of his mind, he heard Matilda scream his name as he felt her juices flood around his cock. He pumped until his climax took him over the edge into utter bliss.

What seemed like minutes later, but was only about thirty seconds, Ioan rolled to his side and pulled a sleeping Matilda into his arms—and held tight. He would never let her go; the possessive part of him had taken over.

Nothing or no one would ever take her away from him. He would care for her for the rest of their lives. Ioan glanced at his wife in awe. He leaned forward and brushed a kiss on her cheek. Ioan laid back down, closed his eyes, and fell asleep.

Knock! Knock!

Ioan shot up from where he laid with Matilda draped across him. Except for the rude awakening, it felt rather amazing to have her in his arms. He dislodged himself from the tangle of limbs on the bed.

He noticed his banyan had been placed on the back of one of the chairs in front of the fireplace. He hurriedly put the article of clothing on and opened the door.

"It's about time you answered the door," James teased him.

Ioan rolled his eyes at his friend's facetiousness.

"I am not going to talk about it with you. What do you need?"

"Access to the 'library' and the records." James smiled.

Ioan glanced at the grandfather clock standing sentry in the hall. "At three o'clock in the morning? Are you insane?"

"No, just can't sleep. I would much rather do something productive."

"And I would much rather be cuddled up with my wife." Ioan smiled back at James. Ioan walked over to a small writing desk near one of the large floor-to-ceiling windows—pulled out a piece of vellum, a quill, and ink—and wrote the combination for the safe, which was the size of a large room, for James.

"Memorize this, then burn it." Ioan handed the page to his friend. An odd feeling of this happening before coursed through him. "James, be careful." With a lift of his head, Ioan watched as James strode away.

Ioan tried like hell to get back to sleep, but was unable to. There was too much weighing on him—a puzzle needing solving, a murderer to catch, and an estate to manage. With help from his friends and Matilda, he would piece together what happened—he was sure of it.

He was glad that he told his valet to put out his clothes the day before. He strode into his changing room and dressed for the day before going to his study.

He was not expecting Finn and Andrew to be up looking through the papers stacked up high on the desk.

"Did you do nothing before you came to London?" Finn glanced up at him from the pile of paper he was going through.

"I tried not to. The numbers made no sense to me. I was going to find someone to do it for me—a man of all work." Ioan knew that his friends knew about his problems with numbers and mathematics. He could memorize numbers, but he couldn't make them work when it came to organizing the accounts for the estate.

"Would you like me to ask Beth to look into these for you?" Andrew asked as he lowered himself to sit in one of the chairs in front of the large desk.

"I just may—if she isn't busy helping with the investigation." Ioan steepled his fingers under his chin in contemplative thought.

"Ioan, did you know that some of these correspondences are in code?" Finn asked while reading one of the missives. "Nothing makes sense, but it looks like a code we used earlier in the war with France."

"When Matilda wakes, we will ask her. She is our code specialist. She has a near perfect memory for anything she reads. She was also in charge of coding and decryption for Tarleton." Ioan chortled when he saw the dumbfounded looks on his friends' faces.

"I shouldn't have been surprised." Finn paused in his reading.

"Beth was part of the organization once upon a time, as well." Andrew glanced up from what he was doing.

Ioan could believe that Andrew's incredibly intelligent wife had once been one of Tarleton's minions. He had to laugh at his own thoughts.

A silhouette of a woman came into the library, hands on her hips. "I heard my name. What are you talking about?" Elizabeth asked as she crossed over to where her husband was sitting.

"T-that you had worked for Tarleton once upon a time," Andrew replied.

"I see. That was a very long time ago…" Elizabeth mused.

Ioan smiled. He could imagine Elizabeth being a spy. He had always thought the woman had many secrets. Obviously, she had told his friend many of them—but not all of them.

"Let's get to work," a soft voice came from the doorway.

Ioan nodded as Matilda crossed the room towards him and picked up one of the missives.

Chapter Sixteen

MATILDA HELD THE piece of vellum in her hands as shock went through her. Her hand shook, tears welling up in her eyes. She didn't understand. She searched her memories. Then it clicked.

"What's wrong?" Matilda felt Ioan's arms wrap around her.

"This is my cypher and my handwriting. I didn't..." Matilda couldn't hold back the tears any longer. She truly hadn't realized who she was corresponding with, since they all used code names and she had never been privy to who the names were. "I never knew who they were. They were faceless names," she bawled.

It shouldn't have hit her so hard, yet it did. Matilda knew in that moment that she would do anything in her power to get the person who was responsible for murdering Ioan's family.

Then some fragments of ideas took root in her mind. The men were poisoned. Typical, that would be the easiest way to assassinate a person who was protected by loyal highlanders. Unfortunately, most poisons that she knew of had an odor or taste to them. How would the assassin disguise that?

Matilda would have to do some research. Luckily, she had all the books she would need at her fingertips—since they were in a library, after all. She chastised herself for trying to be silly in a serious moment—even if it was just herself privy to the silliness.

"Ioan, where do you keep your books on herbology?" She strode toward one of the large bookcases.

"To your left, second shelf from the top. They are all alphabetical by subject."

Matilda shouldn't have been surprised. Her uncle's library was just as meticulous in its organization.

"Why?"

As she reached to grab a book, Matilda replied, "You said that your family may have been poisoned. If that was the case, they would have had to have contact with it or ingested it through food or drink."

Matilda glanced up in time to see Ioan nod in agreement. Time was of the essence—and they were slowly running out. The same person who murdered her husband's family may be after him next.

Voices? Why was he hearing—oh, that was due to him getting caught in Tarleton's decoy study. He should have known better. He couldn't blame himself for bad information—or could he?

The man he remembered from before, Elijah, stormed into the room. "What is your name? And who do you work for?"

"My name is Mr. Black. I work for whoever pays the most." Black forced himself to stay calm. If he let his nerves get the best of him, it could cause problems in the future.

"I think you're lying to me. You are too scrawny to be who you say you are. I have met with Mr. Black many times. You are not him. Who are you?"

Black took a moment to come up with an answer before all his secrets came out. His older, much meaner, brother was the man Elijah would have met with. He was running out of time. Black could tell a version of the truth, but he would still need sanctuary from the nightmare he had landed into.

"The man you met was my brother, Silas." Black sighed.

"You were sent because you were nimbler on your feet? Or

were you a decoy?"

It was getting harder and harder to stay in character. He had trained incredibly meticulously for this role. There was nothing for it—

"I am lighter of foot and nimbler. I can get into places that he could not. I don't know if I am a decoy or not. Neither does my brother," he shouted, realizing too late what he had done.

The look on Elijah's face was one of pure shock. Black had to hold back the mirth bubbling up inside him.

"You're a—woman!" The man finally forced out the words.

"I am," she whispered. "My name is Amelia Black. There isn't much more I can tell you."

The man named Elijah glanced at her. "Who hired you?"

Amelia shook her head. "I don't know his name. He paid me one hundred guineas and said that he would give me another hundred upon completion of the job."

"What was your job?"

"To steal the cypher," she replied.

"The cypher? Damn it all to hell!" the man bellowed. "What was your brother's mission?"

"He told me that he would be back in a couple of weeks. He said something about the heather looking pleasant this time of year."

At that moment, Amelia knew that something was drastically wrong. She had been a decoy, after all. With everything wrong in her life, she had to admit to being an honorable thief. She never harmed anyone. She did what she was paid for, retrieving "misplaced" objects. She wasn't into hurting people or animals.

"I need sanctuary." The words rushed out of her mouth.

Elijah glanced at her and nodded. "Of course, are you prepared to tell us everything?"

Amelia nodded in agreement.

"I need to hear the words from you, my dear."

"Yes, I will tell you what I know, but wouldn't it be more prudent to send a messenger post haste to the Scottish Highlands?"

"A messenger was sent the moment you told me about your brother. Hopefully, he can make it there before your brother has time to assassinate my colleagues."

Not long later, Amelia was sitting in a comfortable high-backed chair in front of a roaring fire, sipping a cup of hot tea. She felt as if most of her worries had been taken from her shoulders. For the first time in a long time, she felt comfortable in her own skin.

That didn't mean that Amelia still didn't have secrets. She had plenty of them. Maybe one day she would tell someone. But not just anyone. The person would have to be special. If she told the wrong person, her life—and that of her brother's, would be forfeit.

"Miss Amelia, Master Elijah is back from his errand and would like a word with you. If you would follow me." The footman motioned to the back of the house to a room that must be the man's office.

Once inside, she marveled in the masculine furnishings. The beautiful man behind the desk glanced at her. She watched as a myriad of different emotions flitted across his face.

"You must be feeling more yourself, Miss Amelia." The man stood and sketched a small bow.

"As well as I can be in the situation I have found myself in, Elijah," she replied.

Amelia sat down in one of the chairs across from him and waited.

"I've asked for your presence because of some interesting news I have just come across." Elijah stared at her, making Amelia feel unbalanced and awkward. "Your brother is a wanted man in several countries. The United States, France, Spain, and Portugal—all for spy related charges. What do you know about this?"

Amelia gasped. She hadn't known what her brother had gotten into or who he worked for. *Damn him,* she cursed in her mind.

"I am not aware of his activities when he isn't at home. He keeps most of his dealings away from me. I know that someone hired me to steal the cypher, that's all."

Amelia was getting frustrated. Well, beyond frustrated, if she was honest. She could make things right with Whitehall. She couldn't get her life back because she had been caught—her reputation gone in one moment.

"I believe you, I truly do. You don't seem like an assassin, though no one could believe you had it in you to kill someone. The only issue is, I know several women assassins—and they look just as innocent as you. I am sorry, but I can't trust you. When Tarleton returns, I am sure that you will get an appointment with him."

Amelia couldn't hold back her anger. "I am more than my family, sir. When you understand that, I will tell you who my family is. Until then, I am going to the library to read." She stomped out of the study with her fists clutched.

"Whatever you do, Miss Amelia, you better not leave this house," Elijah sneered back at her.

ELIJAH HAD AN idea of who Amelia was, but it would have been impossible. The girl looked enough like his own mother it was uncanny. Elijah Hutchinson was the last remaining member of his family—or so he presumed. He was the Marquis of Heathfield and a very distant relation to Lord Tarleton.

Damn and blast! Most of his family had died in a fire. The family seat had been razed to the ground with all the family and servants still inside—the doors chained closed. He was lucky—if he felt inclined to believe. He had been at a friend's house for the holidays.

His sister and younger brother, by just minutes, had been murdered along with the rest of the family or, at least, that's what he was told. Until now.

How did they escape? Where had they been all these years? He needed the answer, and yet, Amelia hadn't said anything— and probably wouldn't until he started trusting her a bit more.

Elijah sighed and hoped that he hadn't gotten his hopes up.

OUT ON THE high seas, Tarleton and Percy were on their way back to England. Another goose chase ended with nothing. He hoped to get more information, at the least, but he was losing confidence and that the young man he was trying to find may—in fact—be dead. Tarleton didn't want to admit defeat, and yet, it was staring him in the face.

"Where did you get the information, Percy?" Tarleton asked.

"The usual informants. Though, I think we need to rethink who we use as informants from now on." Percy replied.

Tarleton nodded. He had been thinking much the same thing. Their informants were no longer reliable or trustworthy. He knew of some more reliable people who could help them in the future—and they would be loyal to him. He may just enlist the help of Rathdrum's men. It would do them good.

Tarleton would speak with the duke about that after he got off the boat.

Chapter Seventeen

MATILDA, STILL FEELING guilty over the deaths of her husband's family, sat in a highbacked chair near the ornate fireplace in Ioan's study. The men were milling about holding papers and speaking about theories while she was debating facts in her mind. She couldn't base a theory from suppositions. All she needed was in the coded messages.

"I need all the coded messages with me," Matilda blurted out as she thought to herself. She was shocked when she found multiple messages in her lap. Continuing with her thoughts, she ordered, "Any notes pertaining to the research, please hand them over to Ioan. Any financial books and records, please hand them over to Beth." She wasn't normally the one to take charge of a situation, but she needed to delegate the workload or they wouldn't get anything done.

Somewhere in the distance, Matilda heard one of the men whisper, "She surely can be intimidating."

She chuckled to herself when Ioan replied, "Have you not met her uncle?"

"Her uncle?"

"My uncle and godfather is Lord Tarleton. In public, he is my godfather and has taken care of me since my mother died," she said as methodically as she could. She didn't know what Uncle Anthony would want her to disclose about their relationship.

Matilda surveyed the room and saw the gentlemen nod. She

knew that Beth knew since they had been close since they were children.

"None of you seem surprised."

"We are very observant, Your Grace. We noticed at the Haversham Ball," Phineas explained.

Matilda remembered the men circled around the duke at the ball. It was a month ago, but she still felt her cheeks flush when she thought of the one waltz she had with Ioan.

Matilda stood, taking a stack of missives with her. "I am going to the music room," she said as she strode off.

IOAN KNEW WHAT Matilda would be doing, and based on Elizabeth's reaction—she knew also.

"We need to wait a bit; Matilda does her best thinking while playing a piano." Elizabeth clapped her hands in delight.

"Why is my wife carrying on like a small child?" Andrew asked.

"You will have to be patient. Your patience will be pleasantly rewarded!" Elizabeth shouted.

Ioan couldn't agree more. He knew that his friends would be shocked. Ioan glanced at his pocket watch—it had been ten minutes since Matilda left the room. He nodded at Elizabeth.

"Follow the music." Elizabeth grabbed Andrew's hand and dragged him out of the study and down the hall.

"Follow them." Ioan chuckled.

James and Finn followed him from the room, hearing the enchanting melodies. Ioan could see some of his servants lining the halls, enjoying the recital.

The tone of the music changed as she played her favorite Beethoven piece. Matilda must be frustrated, Ioan thought to himself.

As soon as she completed the "Moonlight Sonata", he heard

her switch to the piece he wanted to try. The themes resonated with every part of him. Soon he caught himself swaying to the beat being played by the bass notes.

To his left, Ioan could see the tears falling from Elizabeth's eyes. James, Finn, and Andrew were transfixed, and Ioan couldn't help but smile at the spectacle.

Moments later, Ioan eased close enough to Matilda to sit on the bench next to her. He watched as her fingers gracefully skipped across the keys, each stroke pausing slightly. He knew, at that moment, that she knew that he was there with her—which had him wondering to himself why he was jealous of the piano keys. Ioan continued to enjoy Matilda's performance, memorizing each chord—every note.

All too soon, the music stopped. Matilda's hands came to rest on the tops of her legs and she turned her head toward him. Ioan could feel peace rolling off her in waves.

"Do you remember the name of the man that Uncle Anthony is trying to locate?"

"He never said, but he did say he was the heir to a dukedom and the duke was in bad health," Ioan responded.

"James, did you find anything?"

Ioan turned towards James and found his friend staring blankly at him.

"…I thought he was dead," James chanted repeatedly. "My friend's brother was supposed to have died in a fire. Elijah was the only one, except for his grandfather, to have survived the fire. They were both away from the house. Every door had been chained to keep the family inside." James' eyes filled with tears. "We had no reason to believe that he had survived."

"Elijah? As in Elijah Hutchinson?" Ioan asked.

"The very same. He works for Tarleton, something like his second-in-command. I don't know what his title is, but he would be in line to the dukedom—since the fire wiped out the entire family. The brother may be the elder, though Elijah always claimed that he was—they are not identical twins." James couldn't stop there. "I was friends with both of them when we were young boys."

Ioan couldn't imagine what his friend was going through.

"He is correct. I had codenames for enemy operatives. Mr. Black was a spy for a network based in London, the Shadows. We never got a positive identification on Mr. Black. He was a ghost. He was a master of disguises." Matilda stood up from the bench.

"The letters? They had all that in code?" James asked.

"No, the code is based off the lyrics to the song I just played. I wrote the piece. Only myself and your father," she glanced at Ioan, "knew the code. Uncle Anthony didn't want to know it in case he was tortured by the enemy."

"Could this 'Mr. Black' have something to do with the murder of my family?"

Ioan knew what Matilda would say. It was possible, but based on the fact the three were poisoned—it would most likely be a woman, a scorned lover perhaps.

⫸⫷

MATILDA KNEW THE moment Ioan asked the question that her amazing husband already knew what she would say. It was unlikely Mr. Black did it himself—but it could have been someone under his tutelage, like an apprentice, a woman apprentice.

The old duke had notated something in the code that didn't make sense to her. Something about the princess and the prince? She would need to go back over her code.

"My dear, its nearly time to break our fast, then we can go back over what we have found." Ioan urged her to the door and motioned the others to join them.

Matilda felt Ioan's hand at the small of her back. She craved her husband's touch and she cherished it even more. *Maddy, take your mind away from the marriage bed and onto the clues in front of you!*

ANTHONY ALIGHTED FROM his carriage to the decoy house he had made into a safe house. He had dropped Percy off at the townhouse in Mayfair and had stopped by his Whitehall office just to find a note from Elijah Hutchinson. The man hadn't gone into specifics, but he needed to get to the house as soon as he could.

Here he was, stepping down from his carriage after spending several weeks on a ship with nothing to do but spend most of it hurling everything he ate off the side of the vessel.

Anthony glanced at the house, noticing that candles were still lit in the library. Since he knew that Elijah preferred the study, Anthony couldn't make sense of what was in front of him. He opened the door to find Elijah storming toward him.

"Follow me. There is something, ahem, someone, you need to see," Elijah commanded.

Normally, Anthony would have berated his friend—and cousin—for daring to tell him what to do, but he was intrigued. He didn't know what he thought he would see as he strode into the library—it wasn't what he saw.

His mouth dropped open. "Is that—?"

Elijah nodded his head. "I believe so; she looks too much like my mother not to be. She said she has an older brother."

"Where have they been?" Anthony croaked as emotion welled within him.

The last time he had seen Amy, he had been at his grandfather's ducal estate. Amy had been six years old. Her dark hair had been curly and usually tied in a cue or in plaits. Her light blue eyes had shimmered with mirth. She had followed him everywhere, wanting to play with the boys since there were no girls nearby.

The woman sitting in the chair reading was enchanting even though she was wearing britches.

"Amy?" Anthony called out, hoping the woman in front of him would react to the pet name he had given her when she was younger. The woman gasped. Anthony rushed to her and pulled her into his arms. "We thought you were dead." He held onto her as tight as he could, trying to keep his emotions at bay. No matter how hard he tried, tears still streamed down his face.

What seemed like hours later, Anthony was finally able to get his erstwhile emotions under control. There was something about the situation that seemed wrong. How did Amy, or Amelia—as she preferred to be called—escape the fire? Were the youngest Hutchinson siblings abducted? There were too many questions and not enough answers.

"Do we know where Mr. Black has tarried off to?" Anthony asked Elijah.

"On the clues Amelia gave us, I am assuming the Highlands. She was paid to steal the cypher…"

Anthony's head jerked in response. Great God Almighty! Fuck! What was the man in the Highlands for? Then his mind settled on Matilda and who she had just married. No! Mr. Black somehow knew that the cypher wasn't just a code, it was a person.

He felt sick to his stomach. It wasn't until he felt arms wrap around him that he realized he had panicked. He never had a case of the vapors before. At the thought of his only family in danger, he couldn't hold himself together.

Then he turned his mind toward the small arms that were wrapped around him—Amy. She had grounded him. She had kept him from making a spectacle of himself. He stayed where he stood, in the arms of a woman he had long since thought died.

"Anthony?"

"Yes, Amy?"

"I am glad I tried to steal from your house." Amelia chuckled.

"I am torn, angel. If you hadn't, we would have never known you were alive. Now that I know, you are going to stay here where I can protect you."

Anthony couldn't worry about Amy and Matilda; well, he could and would, but he didn't trust anyone else with Amy's safety other than himself and Elijah.

"Of course, I will remain here. I have nowhere else to go. I need to be able to do something while I am here." Amelia turned so that she was facing him.

Anthony couldn't have her working for him until he knew he could trust her with his secrets. He didn't know who she worked for and wouldn't until he knew about her training.

"We will see about what we can do about keeping you busy," Anthony said as he held onto her—as if she might fly away at any moment.

Anthony tucked her in closer to him and gently kissed the top of her head.

Chapter Eighteen

MATILDA WOKE UP to the sun shining through the window and a fire roaring in the fireplace. She stretched and found an extra arm around her middle. Ioan was still with her. It wasn't like they hadn't spent all night, all day, and most of the next night working through the information that they had gleaned from her coded messages.

At around two o'clock in the morning, no one was able to work and they had all gone to their rooms for some much needed rest.

"Go back to sleep," Ioan grumbled from his place on the bed.

Matilda smiled. "There are far too many things to do, though."

"Yes, there are." The man dared to smile wickedly at her.

Matilda pulled up from the bed and strode around it to lean down and press a kiss upon her husband's lips—or, at least, that's the way it started, yet wasn't the way it ended. The kiss deepened. A battle of tongues, lips, and teeth ensued.

Ioan pulled her over him so that Matilda was straddling him, his cock settled into the 'v' of her thighs. The kiss continued, scorching her, sending her into a roaring, burning frenzy.

Her mind was no longer on the day's work, but the pleasure she found in her husband's arms—or other parts of his anatomy. Her body gyrated against his large cock, needing what he could give her, needing the release.

Knock, knock!

Damn and blast! Matilda cursed to herself. She tried to push herself off Ioan, but based on previous experiences, she rolled off him and pulled the bedspread up to her chin in time for Ioan to bid the intruder to enter the room.

The doorknob turned and—James peeked his head in.

"Are you lovebirds awake yet?"

"Give us a moment and we will be down," Ioan replied.

Matilda groaned and pulled the blanket above her head.

"Don't hide, love. You are beautiful. You are desirable and I need you. But—our friends require our presence in the dining room." Ioan pulled back the blanket and gracefully strode toward his dressing room. Matilda couldn't keep her eyes off him as she tracked him across the room. He was beautiful, even when he claimed he wasn't.

Matilda grabbed the blanket, wrapped herself in it, and raced into the duchess' dressing room where her lady's maid had been waiting.

"Your Grace," the maid addressed her.

"You've already drawn a bath, thank you!" Matilda watched as the maid's face flushed in pleasure. She knew in that moment that they would be fast friends.

Within moments, Matilda was soaking in the luxurious bath as her lady's maid washed her exposed skin—until she could smell the clean scent of lavender in the air.

"If Your Grace would step out of the bath, I can get your hair put into a neat plait before you go down to break your fast," the maid said in her Scottish brogue.

Matilda nodded. She didn't have time for a more complicated coiffure—a plait would do for now. Maybe, once she came back from breakfast—that was, if the others didn't want to get back to work right away. Anything was possible.

As her lady's maid finished with her hair and helped her dress, Matilda left the room and took her time finding the dining room. She surveyed the halls—tapestries hung, telling stories of long ago battles. Portraits hung of people she didn't know, but she knew they had been ancestors of Ioan's. She captured the sights in her mind's eye and continued to stroll down the hall in complete awe.

Too soon, she came to the dining room. Everyone was seated around the large table. James and Finn were arguing over something in the *Edinburgh Post*, most likely to do with tensions growing in Ireland. Elizabeth and Andrew were leafing through one of Ioan's account books while Ioan nibbled on a fresh pastry of unknown variety.

Matilda took a seat next to Ioan. The man squeezed her leg in welcome. Need, unrelenting need, raced through her. Slightly embarrassed, Matilda sought Ioan's eyes.

Ioan leaned down to her and whispered in her ear, "We will finish what we started after you get something to eat."

James and Finn glanced up at that moment, as if they had heard Ioan speak, and Matilda blushed even more. Both men wiggled their eyebrows at her and chuckled, making her flush more than she already was.

"Don't let them rile you. They mean no harm," Ioan said while sending a menacing glare toward his friends.

Matilda knew that James and Finn were being playful, but being new to bed sport, she was bashful, let alone her complexion increased the chance of her blushing.

"I think I will go to the music room once I am finished. I would like to spend some time with the harp and the piano, if I may?" Matilda dipped her head down. "I have been learning Mrs. Maddox's song. I would like to make it perfect for her."

Ioan couldn't find fault with her wanting to do something different than what he wanted. He wouldn't change a thing about her. Her pixie-like personality made it hard to keep her in one place very long, except for when she was at the piano. Then she let out all her emotions and everyone around her could feel what she felt—and it was beautiful.

Ioan wanted to go with her, but felt that she needed time to herself more than an audience. Even coming to that conclusion, Ioan stopped by his study to grab a few sheets of vellum, a quill, some ink to write out some clues while listening to her play, as well as some of the notes that his father had left him as clues—then he continued to the music room where he heard her do the scales, which he knew was just how she warmed up her fingers.

As Matilda started playing in earnest, Ioan sat down in one of the ornate chairs by the windows overlooking the gardens. The view induced him to jot down some ideas, bringing him back to the deaths of his family. The gardens here at the clan seat were extensive. Maybe? He wrote down to make a list of all plants on the grounds. Something on the grounds could have been used to poison his family.

Then Ioan flipped through the notes he had found on the desk. Not the coded missives, but the notes his father had taken during the research he had done for Tarleton. A phrase stood out to him, something in Latin. He should have studied his Latin more in school—he had much preferred Greek to Latin.

Thank goodness he had the presence of mind to bring something to write on and with or his thoughts would have scattered, and trying to remember anything, would have been—he shut down that thought. He had an excellent memory for anything he had read, but not so much for random thoughts that chose to come into his mind.

Maybe, just maybe, his random thoughts would provide insight to the murder.

ANTHONY WAS IN a race against time. An assassin was on his way to kill his niece, or at the very least, abduct her. The man already had a two day head start. Fuck! Even with riding, he would have to stop to switch horses, which would get him to Rathdrum's Scottish seat way too late. Even the fastest ship couldn't beat the man.

He was completely beside himself. He would make his way up to Scotland and hope that the duke and his people could protect Matilda in the meantime. That's all he could do—no, he could pack up and have the trunks readied for a trip to Scotland.

"Elijah, get yourself ready and have a footman go to the wharf. We are going to Edinburgh," Anthony commanded.

He didn't wait to see if his friend had done as he had bid as he stormed from the room.

"Anthony! I want to come with you. He is my brother; I know how to appease him without bloodshed." Amelia stared at him from where she stood at the bottom of the stairs.

"Very well, Amy, but you stay with me," Anthony ground out. He would not lose her again—ever.

It was at that very moment that he had to admit to himself that he had feelings for his little sprite. He would never let anyone take her from him again. He knew, in his mind, that he was being possessive. He was very rarely this way over those who were close to him; that had changed dramatically with Amelia's return.

He pushed the thought away as he climbed the rest of the stairs to pack his trunks, again, for another journey—this one time to save Matilda from a mad man.

Chapter Nineteen

AS EVERY NEW day began, Matilda was out of bed before the cock crowed. She enjoyed watching the sunrise from the large windows in the music room, with a steaming cup of chocolate warming her hands. She never stepped outside unless someone from the staff or Ioan came with her.

At that moment, a flash of color flitted across the moor. Whatever it was caught her eye and she tried to track it, but it had gone out of her line of sight. In the pit of her stomach, she knew something wasn't right.

Matilda turned her head for a moment and witnessed the most alarming sight. A large man was standing outside the door, trying to open it but couldn't because of the locks. Then, the man bent his elbow, as if to break the glass.

She must have been having a nightmare. She heard a scream, not realizing it was coming from her. She heard a stampede of feet race toward the room. Her panic gradually eased as the man ran off and the household staff rushed into the room.

At the sight, Matilda couldn't help but laugh. The cook had a cast iron pan in her hands. A footman held a golf club. Another held a cricket bat. It wouldn't have mattered if the man had a gun, but her husband's people would be there to protect her.

Out of the silence, a horrible, terrifying sound came from within the house. "Donnae worry, lass. Duncan sounded the alarm." The cook glanced at her.

"What is that horrible sound?" She cringed as the sound got closer.

"'Tis the bagpipes, lass. Have ye never heard them played?"

She had heard of the instrument, but had thought they had been banned after the 1746 uprising. The caterwauling of the instrument gave her a horrible case of the megrims. She could feel the blood pound in her head. She felt faint and saw black dots in her vision.

"For all that is holy—stop playing. The wee lass doesnae look well." The cook bellowed over the noise, enhancing the pain even more as black took over her sight.

IOAN WOKE UP to the alarming sound of bagpipes being played inside his house. The only time he allowed anyone to play the outlawed pipes, notably the most annoying instrument on earth, was when there was a threat.

As quickly as he could, he threw on a pair of britches and a shirt—and raced down the stairs. He followed the sound of the bagpipes then came across a large line of staff trying to get into the music room; every man and woman had something heavy in their hands—weapons.

"What is going on here?" Ioan bellowed over the panicked noise around him.

The butler wielding a butcher's knife turned toward him. "We heard Her Grace scream. We brought our weapons and prepared for battle."

Ioan surveyed the room and nearly died laughing at the sight. His staff wielded brooms, pitchforks, pots and pans, anything that was heavy enough to inflict as much pain as possible. Then his eyes came to a halt when he saw Matilda cradled in Cook's arms. Ioan pushed his way through the throng of people as he raced to her.

"What happened?"

"She had quite the shock, Master Ioan. Something scared our English Rose and then the bagpipes—" Cook glanced down at the younger woman. "I saw her knees buckle, and I caught her before she could hit the ground."

Ioan was thankful for Cook's quick thinking and reflexes. "Thank you." He took Matilda into his arms. "Please go back to bed and you can all take the morning off."

The sound of joy coming from the staff echoed off the walls as Ioan carried Matilda back to their rooms. He needed answers from her. What did she see that spooked her? Matilda wasn't a woman who would scare easily.

A small tingle raced up his spine, as if someone was watching them from the shadows. He would need to tell his friends and set up a watch. They had a problem—an incredibly big problem.

Matilda was still out when he got to his rooms. Her face was unusually pale. That wasn't like her, at all. Ioan placed Matilda on the counterpane and hoped that he could awaken her.

"Darling, wake up," he whispered in her ear.

With a start, she sat up straight and screamed. Ioan didn't understand what was happening to her. She kept screaming and all he could do was hold her, hoping that she would recognize him.

Then, moments later, the room was quiet and Matilda blinked her eyes at him.

"What happened?" Matilda asked as he helped lower her back against the pillows.

"Something scared you and you fainted into Cook's arms," Ioan replied.

"It wasn't something, but a very large someone. He tried to come through the door in the music room. I didn't get a good look at his face." She pouted.

Ioan couldn't hold back the mirth as he watched the expression on his beloved wife's face. "Darling, I will have men search the moor, and hopefully, they will find this person. We will also always keep a guard near you."

Ioan didn't know if his words would comfort Matilda, but he vowed to keep her safe no matter what; he prayed, for the first time, that God would keep his wife safe.

"Thank you."

Ioan watched as Matilda slipped back to sleep.

TARLETON, ACTING AS the spy master and not the scared uncle with everything to lose, raced for Scotland along the old North Road. It was the quickest way. He figured that Amy was safest with Elijah on a ship bound for Edinburgh rather than on a horse racing toward who knew what.

He had stopped at many of the posting houses along the route where he changed horses and kept riding. He stopped at night to get food in his belly and a couple hours of sleep before continuing.

On the fifth day, he sighed in relief when he saw the façade of Ioan's manor house. He couldn't believe that he had made it in as short of time as he had. Now, to wait for Amy and Elijah since they were coming by boat. He worried about his old friends—not knowing what kind of traps Mr. Black had waiting for them.

Tarleton couldn't worry about them when his niece was in trouble. He mentally shook himself. He needed to keep himself calm and collected.

As he came to the circular drive, the door flew open and a godawful sound came from inside. What was going on? The only other time he had heard the bagpipes played was at the same house, but another clan came without prior notice and the duke's men considered it an attack. He didn't understand clan histories, but it nearly caused an outright battle in the moor in the front of the ducal manse.

It was the most asinine thing he had ever witnessed. No man

held a sword or gun—but pitchforks, hoes, and shovels. Anthony couldn't help but laugh at the spectacle.

Unfortunately, this time, there was no battle, which made Tarleton wonder what in the hell was happening.

"My lord! It is nice—um, well—that you are here. His Grace will need your assistance." The butler urged him through the door as the bagpipes stopped playing.

Anthony followed the butler to the ducal chambers.

"Their Graces are inside, my lord."

He opened the door and saw a sight that nearly had him running to Matilda's side. "What happened?" Anthony pinned Ioan with a glare.

"A big man tried to get into the house and scared Matilda. Which cause the alarm to sound. We need to find out who it was. Though, I am thankful that you are here—why are you here?"

Anthony ignored the question as he sidled up to where Matilda was perched on the bed. He cupped her cheek. It nearly broke him seeing her like this.

"A man known as Mr. Black, an assassin, has been hired to take Matilda by force. I am here to stop him from doing so. I have a friend coming to help. They should be here soon."

"We could use the help." Ioan nodded in agreement.

Anthony couldn't stand still. Mr. Black was still out there, planning God knew what—and his team was out there somewhere. He hated waiting. He couldn't stand the unknown—which was ironic since he dealt with the unknown every day.

"My lord?" the butler said, bringing Anthony back to the present.

"Yes?"

"You have visitors."

Anthony jumped from where he sat. Finally! He could feel slightly more at ease. He descended the stairs and saw Amy and Elijah waiting for him. He nodded at Elijah and pulled Amy into his arms.

"How was the trip?"

Amy rolled her eyes. "It's winter on the Atlantic Ocean. How do you think our journey went? Elijah was bent over the stern the entire way. While I spent every day in my cabin wishing I could go out on deck."

Anthony turned toward Elijah, who still looked a bit green.

"I had the same problem going across the channel." Anthony cuffed Elijah on the shoulder and chuckled at his moan of pain. "Apparently, someone also got battered against the rails."

Amy giggled and Anthony promised himself that he would spend eternity making her laugh—just so he could hear the sound. What was he saying to himself? Anthony had been reintroduced to Amy just a few weeks ago and two of those weeks were spent apart.

Yet, he couldn't keep his heart from feeling what it felt. Even as a young man, Anthony had felt a deep kinship toward Amy. He thought it inappropriate at the time—and then the fire, thinking she had died…

"Let's get you both freshened up—then we have work to do. Your brother has already been here once and was unsuccessful." Anthony heard a small gasp.

"You know who the man was?" Matilda asked from behind him.

Holy hell! He needed to explain to her what was going on.

"Anthony, is that Athena's daughter?" Elijah asked in shock.

Anthony rolled his eyes toward the ceiling, hoping that God would deliver him from the coming crisis.

Chapter Twenty

I OAN HAD NOTICED that Matilda had snuck out of bed several minutes after the fact. He ambled his way down the stairs, following the sound of a heated conversation—and some of the voices he had not recognized.

As he approached the hall, Ioan took in the scene. Tarleton was holding a young woman in his arms, another man stood with his jaw open wide enough it almost reached the floor, and Matilda stood with her hands on her hips. If the scene was happening anywhere but his front hall, he would have given into the mirth bubbling inside of him.

Then he saw something truly terrifying—it was as if the devil had taken refuge in Matilda's body. If one single glance could kill, every man, woman, child, and beast would have been ferried to the afterlife. Luckily, he was there to save the day—or, at least, he hoped.

"What is going on here?" Ioan bellowed over the yelling and screaming.

"Uncle Anthony knows who tried to break into the music room but won't tell me. He invited guests and never told us." She then pointed at the poor man who had remained slack-jawed. "And he somehow knew my mother."

Ioan couldn't comprehend everything Matilda said, but got a decent idea. He combed his fingers through his already mussed hair and sighed. There wasn't much for it but to offer what hospitality he could since the staff had been given the morning off.

"Before we speak about what is going on here, you might as well freshen up a bit. There are bedchambers available near Tarleton's." Ioan pulled his pocket watch out and read the time. "We will have luncheon in the dining room at one o'clock. Our whole team will meet and discuss what is happening." Ioan pulled Matilda with him as he turned for the stairs and held her close to him as they climbed the stairs together.

Once they were in their rooms, Ioan pulled Matilda to him and kissed her. Not just any kiss, it was the kiss of dreams. Ioan cherished the moment. His hands roamed every nip and tuck of her body—touching all his favorite places. One dropped down to her hips and traced a path toward her delectable behind. He pinched her and delighted in the squeal that came from her and changed to moans as he massaged the offended muscle.

The other hand caressed her breast. The delicate rose nipple beckoned him, wanting his attention. He broke the kiss, leaving small open-mouthed kisses trailing to her left breast while his hand continued to play with her right. The taste of her was better than any dessert he had ever had. Her skin shivered at his touch; Ioan smiled. He loved how responsive she was, how much she enjoyed being pleasured and how much she enjoyed giving it in return.

He took the rose-colored peak and nipped it before pulling it into his mouth. The sounds she was making nearly hurtled him into his own climax before he even got inside her.

Good lord! He needed her. He needed everything she could give him—especially her heart and soul. He let go of her nipple and kissed his way back up her body as he positioned himself to take her. His need overwhelmed him as he thrust into her.

MATILDA NEEDED THE connection to Ioan, and when he thrust into her, her heart nearly burst in ecstasy. She couldn't imagine a world where Ioan wasn't with her. She ached to tell him how she felt.

Matilda couldn't help rocking against Ioan as he continued to thrust into her body. She wanted him to never stop. That was, until she moved her hand between them and touched the nubbin between her legs. A moan broke forth from her lips.

"Please—" She begged for release.

Ioan must have known what she wanted because, moments later, he was pounding her into the feather mattress and she was screaming his name at the top of her voice.

Matilda felt Ioan slide out of her and he pulled her into him.

"We have an hour before we need to be downstairs," Ioan whispered in her ear.

Matilda shivered. She was overly sensitive to touch; she always was after lovemaking. She didn't understand it, but she knew that it made Ioan smile—reaching far into his eyes.

Moments later, Matilda glanced over to the ornate clock on the table next to the bed where she laid cuddled into Ioan. "Ioan, we need to go downstairs. I am interested to hear what Uncle Anthony has to say."

Sure, she wanted to know why Uncle Anthony was here and why he brought guests, but she wanted to stay where she was, lounging next her husband in the afterglow of lovemaking. Apparently, Ioan felt the same as he pulled her closer to him and kissed the top of her head.

"I suppose. The sooner we discover why Tarleton is here, the sooner we can come back here." He kissed her from her shoulder up to her neck.

"That wasn't fair, Your Grace," Matilda proclaimed as she crawled out of the bed and to the vanity to straighten herself up. She focused for a moment on Ioan through the mirror. The man tracked her every movement. Matilda smiled at him as he also crawled out of the bed and made sure that he was presentable, as well.

⇝⇝⇝✺⇜⇜⇜

ANTHONY WAS IMPATIENTLY waiting for the others to join him. He knew that his niece was always, predictably, late. He knew that Phineas would be arriving momentarily—he was always punctual; if he was late to a meeting, he was dead. James was a military man and would be punctual—speak of the man, he strode into the formal dining room as if summoned.

Anthony had to give himself credit for reading people so easily. As he applauded himself—Phineas, Amy, and Elijah strolled into the room. They were now waiting on Ioan and Matilda.

When the couple finally arrived, they all sat down to an odd luncheon of cold meat and cheese that someone—probably Phineas, who had Cook wrapped around his finger—had procured as a mid-morning meal.

"Now that we are all here, what is going on?" Matilda held his eyes in an unholy glare.

"I don't know about you, Tarleton, but that glare Matilda is giving you would make the best spy in the world give up his secrets!" Phineas proclaimed from the opposite side of the table.

"There is a threat to Matilda," Anthony capitulated. "A man, codenamed Mr. Black, is after the cypher and will abduct Matilda to get it."

He heard Matilda gasp—more out of shock than fear since he knew his niece so well; he could tell the difference.

"Was he the man that tried to break into the house?" she asked.

"We believe so. If the man is who we think he is, you are in danger."

"Who is he, Uncle Anthony?"

He glanced over at Elijah and Amy. "Their brother, Silas, has been an assassin for the organization known as the Shadows."

The audible gasps from around the table surprised him. The Shadows worked as instigators to most of the riots in England and the Continent. Their leader, codename of The Priest, was privy to many of England's secrets. Anthony had been charged with finding the man. One day soon, that man would show him who he was and he would relish that day for the rest of his life.

"Damn!" Phineas and James said in unison.

Anthony knew that the other men had come across Shadow agents before, but nothing like Silas. "Next time, we won't have the element of surprise. He learned our weaknesses with this failed attempt. He will come back." Anthony surveyed the room. "I was hoping with Amy and Elijah here that we could stop him before he tried doing anything. Unfortunately, that option won't work. Since most of the men are out tracking Silas, it leaves the house unprotected. I would guess that he is here."

Every head around the table jerked toward him. He had worked enough jobs, or missions, in the field that he knew the basic plan Silas thought of using—divide and conquer.

"We need to be vigilant."

"We need to get him out in the open," Elijah commented.

Anthony nodded in agreement. "I agree, but how do we do this without putting Matilda in further danger?"

MATILDA SAT IN her chair at the table, listening to the men decide what they were going to do to protect her. She knew that they meant well, except she had been taught, all her life, how to take care of herself. She had other plans. There was not going to be any way that she would stand behind the men. Oh no! She would not.

Matilda pushed herself up from her chair and put her hand out to tell the men they didn't have to rise from their chairs. She bent close to Ioan and whispered, "I am going to the music room. Please, focus on the issue at hand. I will be safe."

As she walked away, the woman known as Amy followed her out of the room.

"What do you plan on doing, Your Grace?"

"I am planning on taking matters into my own hands. Do you want to join me?"

Matilda watched as Amy gave the question some thought.

"Yes, I think I will. I know my brother very well. Anthony was right, though. Silas may already be in the house. Why do you think I broke away from our overprotective friends?" Matilda flashed Amy a mischievous grin.

"My thoughts exactly. Between the two of us, we can take him." Matilda took the knife from her pocket that she had taken earlier without anyone knowing. Luckily. Uncle Anthony had taught her to throw and fight with knives.

"I believe we had similar thoughts and upbringing." Amy snickered while holding up Elijah's switchblade.

While being partially prepared for battle, Matilda led Amy to the music room.

Chapter Twenty-One

ANTHONY SURVEYED THE room, finding all male faces occupying the space. Well, damn! He would need to have a word with the two women in his life. Though, knowing that he had taught Matilda to fight for protection, he was unsure about Amy.

"When did Amelia sneak away?" Elijah asked.

"The same time Matilda loudly proclaimed her displeasure. I would check your pocket. You might find your switchblade missing." Anthony chuckled. "It seems as if the ladies have plans of their own."

Anthony stared as Elijah searched his pockets, coming up with nothing. "We should learn from this, gentlemen. Our women think we are imbeciles."

Then a sound reached his ears. Crashing and clanking coming from the music room. Matilda! Amy! Anthony sprang into action. He pushed his chair away from the table as he struggled to his feet. He had become complacent, and now Amy and his niece were fighting for their lives.

Thank the lord that he carried multiple weapons on him every moment of every day. Then it dawned on him. Fuck! His little friend swiped several of the smaller knives he had hidden on him. He shook his head and raced to the music room, the rest of the gentlemen following him.

What Anthony saw next would be a subject for entertainment for years to come. Somehow, Matilda and Amy had taken his father's old swords off their decorative shield and were sword fighting, each woman were holding their own, evenly matched. Anthony stood mesmerized by watching the women sword play—and he wasn't the only one.

He knew what they were telling him. That they could fight their own battles, and that they weren't afraid of what was coming. Sure, he knew that they could handle themselves in a situation, but not against a seasoned killer with no conscience—except, maybe, about killing his own family—but Anthony wasn't going to place a bet on that.

IOAN COULDN'T BELIEVE what he was seeing—well, he shouldn't have been surprised seeing who her uncle was. The vision of her crossing blades with Tarleton's friend was wreaking havoc with his baser needs. He knew his wife was independent, but he wanted to be the one to defend her, to be her knight in shining armor. If he saw the scene correctly, Matilda would end up being his—and that didn't faze him, at all.

The clashing of swords came to a halt. Ioan's gaze held Matilda's as her sword was placed back in its holder above the fireplace. He couldn't be prouder of her. He raised his arms a bit as she walked into them.

"We thought that you were fighting to the death. Little did we know that either of you could fight like that. I stand in awe of you." Ioan took a knee and bowed before her—followed by all the other gentlemen, including Tarleton.

"Please rise," Matilda said stoically.

Ioan couldn't be prouder of her. The smile brightening her face spoke of how much she needed the praise.

"Ioan, I think we should let her lead us into battle." James chuckled.

His friends, obviously, wanted to have Matilda usurp him as the leader of their venture, and if it weren't for the beliefs of their peers, he would have stepped aside and let her take the lead. On this mission, though, he thought it may be a great idea.

"We will see. Though, I would agree with you—we need a plan."

The other men nodded in agreement. "Ladies, if you would join us!"

FROM THE SHADOWS of the secret room next to the music room, Silas chuckled to himself. His sister and the cypher had, indeed, given a rather impressive—if not entertaining—fight.

He had taught Amelia how to defend herself. The reality of their life had necessitated it, his need to protect her in any way possible from the man who had made him into the man he was. He wasn't proud of it, but—it was something he was good at.

His gaze moved to Tarleton, his onetime friend turned enemy. Tarleton had his sights on Amelia. Something inside Silas recognized what he saw there and nearly gave up his hiding place. The Priest had told him many things about Tarleton and those who worked for him. The man was adamant that the Shadows were to protect the Crown against all enemies—and Tarleton was the enemy.

Silas barely kept a snarl from escaping his lips—and now, the enemy had his sister...and brother. Fuck! Elijah worked for the bastard. His anger peaked. He could ambush them, but the odds weren't in his favor.

There was only one way to go on. His original plan would have to do. He glanced at his sister; she would be the cypher's shadow for now and until the men thought it to be safe enough to leave her on her own. They would never be safe, he vowed.

Both the duke and Tarleton seemed to be intelligent men and

would know that Silas would always be lurking in the shadows, waiting for the best moment to strike—and strike he would.

Silas sneered. There was one minor adjustment to his plan—he would have to take Amelia, as well. The logistics of the mission needed to be set. The best place to snatch and grab the women would be in the music room and out through the glass door.

The problem would be getting them both. Silas had some thinking to do before he executed the plan.

MATILDA HAD A plan. James had promised to take his sister into Edinburgh for some shopping. Of course, Matilda and Amelia were invited to go with them. They would take the ducal carriage to James' estate to get Gloria. They would speak about the trip openly—since everyone thought that Silas may still be in the house.

The next step would be to use the carriage as the staged ambush site. Then take Silas into custody or take him to Tyburn.

Either way, Silas would get punished for killing peers of the realm and the attempted abduction of two peers—which would mean the man had two options available to him, execution, or a one-way ticket to Australia.

Matilda surveyed the room. The men seemed to agree with her strategy—that was except for Uncle Anthony. He looked conflicted.

"Matilda, can I speak with you in private?"

She watched as Elijah bent toward Uncle Anthony and whispered something in his ear. Matilda didn't like secrets and wouldn't abide them in her house. For this mission to be a success, she needed to have all pertinent information—and if her uncle and Elijah knew something that she didn't, it could be disastrous.

"I have no problem with that, but I would like Elijah to come with us, as well. I don't like secrets, uncle, and I believe I have landed myself in a rather large one."

ANTHONY KNEW THE time would come to explain some things to Matilda, and they would be hard topics. Personally, he never thought he would have to deal with this. Strangely enough, he wished Percy was here to help explain it to her.

"Is there a place that we can have this chat?"

"The parlor would be best. Follow me," Matilda commanded him.

Once they got to the room, Anthony and Elijah took the chairs near the fireplace and waited until Matilda sat down before taking a seat, as well.

"Please, enlighten me to this secret you are worried to tell me, Uncle Anthony." Matilda sat straight in her seat.

Anthony gazed at her. "You are so much like your mother. Athena was beautiful and independent. She was kind. She was also five years my senior. Elijah and Silas would come to our house, occasionally, just to play, or for holidays when we got older." Anthony glanced over at Elijah. "It was that day, the day of the fire, that Elijah was over to our house for the holiday. I remember it as if it was just yesterday." Anthony glanced down at his hands. "Athena was home for the remainder of her pregnancy since your father was on the Continent. She was heavy with child. Elijah and I were fascinated. Her belly danced with your kicks and she let us touch her belly to feel your presence." Tears welled up in his eyes. "It was on this day that she had leaked fluid and she cried in pain. Pure chaos struck the house. The doctor was sent for. *Oh God!*" he shouted. He didn't like talking about the loss of his sister. "It, the birth, was taking too long. Athena was barely hanging on when you came into the world. Moments later, she was gone." Anthony sniffed, took a handkerchief from his pocket, and dabbed at his nose.

"My parents were so lost to their own grief that they had not thought of you. Elijah and I took care of you to the best of our ability.

"You and Athena are the reasons why I went to medical school in Edinburgh," Elijah said.

Anthony noticed the tears welling up in Matilda's eyes and watched as they started to stream down her face. He wished that he could take the pain away from her—he wished he could take the pain away from himself also. He had only been thirteen when Matilda was born. From that day forward, she was Anthony's— her father, through his own grief, had abandoned her to Anthony's care.

"I know where your thoughts are going, Maddy. Your father loves you in his own way. He just doesn't know how to express that love.

"When I was old enough, I took over a group attached to Whitehall, the group that your father was part of. He was not the man he is now. He was still angry—at himself and at God—and hurt. I took over his role in your life and raised you as best as I could."

IT TOOK A while for Matilda to come to grips with what she just learned. She had cried, she had mourned the loss of the mother she never got to know. It wracked her. The pain was so fresh that she couldn't express how she felt. It hurt; there was no other word for the emotional anguish that she felt inside. She would need to take time to get over this new issue, but she knew that with Ioan to help her, she could find herself, once again.

✦

Chapter Twenty-Two

IOAN STOOD OUTSIDE the parlor listening to the conversation through the door. He was shocked at what he had heard, though he shouldn't have been. He had known that Tarleton had raised Matilda from a young age. The rest of it was new.

The door swung open. "Would you like to join us, Your Grace?"

"I will be right in," Ioan replied. He had to laugh at his situation. He had been caught eavesdropping through the door like a wayward child.

As he strode through the door the parlor, he noticed Matilda seated near the fireplace, her eyes red and swollen from crying.

"What did you to do her, Tarleton?" Ioan was furious. His normally sassy wife was a shadow of herself.

"You heard the conversation, Your Grace. Would you be smiling and happy after what you just heard?"

Ioan knew that he would have been inconsolable if he had gotten the news that Matilda had just been given. "No, I would assume not," Ioan replied.

Ioan strode over to Matilda and pulled her into his arms—holding her close. For a moment, he thought that holding her would comfort her, as well as himself. He held her as if she was something fragile. Someone who he held in the highest regard—loved.

When her quiet sobs finally waned, Ioan gazed into her eyes

and held them with his, letting her know that he was there for her. He could understand how she felt. For God's sake, he had just been through something similar with his family. There one moment and gone the next. He knew that there wasn't a word he could say that would take away the grief.

ANTHONY GLANCED OVER at the lovebirds huddled near the fireplace. He wished he hadn't told Matilda about her mother, but he knew how much she hated secrets—and the one he told her was a large one. He turned his head toward Elijah and nodded.

"I don't think that went too horribly bad. It could've been worse—she could blame you for the way things turned out," Elijah spoke.

Anthony thought a moment before replying. "You're right. I should have done it sooner."

"Were you ready for that conversation a year ago?"

He shook his head.

"So, doing it now—when Matilda has her husband for support and family around her—you made the right choice."

"When did you get so wise?" Anthony asked his friend.

"When a certain spy master asked me to join his team in a medical capacity." Elijah smiled.

Anthony grinned. He had needed a doctor on his team—not just for his men, but the women and children they rescued. He would also need one for the Valor and Honor men too. He had a couple of men in mind, but he would need to ask Rathdrum what his needs were for additional men and in what capacity they would work in.

"You seem to be in a world of your own." Elijah's voice broke through Anthony's thoughts.

"I was just pondering the needs of Rathdrum's department and hoping that we can help equip him with the men he needs, including a doctor."

"I know some who were field medics with James' company during the wars. They may be able to be trained to do what I do. I would need several months with them to make sure that they know what I know," Elijah commented.

Anthony pondered what his friend had said. It was true that two of the men he had recommended to the Valor and Honor Team had training, but not the kind that Elijah could provide.

"Would you be able to take the time to train at least one of the men?" Anthony glanced over to his friend.

"I don't see why not. I do need the man to come down to London for a while." Elijah wrung his hands.

"I will speak with Rathdrum, as I said, about that. Since they haven't, technically, hired them yet. I don't foresee it being an issue."

Anthony surveyed around him and felt as if his every movement was being watched. Silas was in the walls somewhere. Damn the man. They would need to implement their plan—and soon.

Chapter Twenty-Three

MATILDA WIPED AWAY the tears that she had shed after hearing the story of her birth. There was nothing she could about it now, but she did understand more about the dynamics between her uncle and her father.

She needed to be strong—not just for herself, but for the team, as well. She wiped the remaining tears from her eyes, stood up, and straightened her shoulders.

"Isn't there something we need to do?" Matilda put her hands on her hips and strode out of the room.

Matilda found the rest of the men and Amelia still in the music room. "We have a plan to enact. James, how long does it take to get to your estate?"

"By carriage? Maybe an hour or two. By horse? Less than that."

"It's too late now to leave. We travel at dawn. If you could have the carriage brought around by ten o'clock. That should give us time to stop by your estate and be well on our way to Edinburgh by early afternoon," Matilda commanded as she rushed to the stairs.

She was a woman on a mission. She was over letting some man kill her people. Matilda raced to her rooms, threw open the door, and didn't know what she could do. Her mind raced, hoping to come up with some conclusion—some hope that she could find a way out of the mess they had all found themselves in.

Matilda did the one thing she had never done—let herself slip. She couldn't control the problem, but Matilda knew that the men had experience in keeping people safe in and out of warfare. Some even had experience in the game of intrigue—because that's what it was, a game.

They would need their combined gifts and experience to bring down the Shadows.

IOAN COULDN'T HELP but love the spitfire that stormed out of the parlor. He loved her mettle—that even in her lowest moment, she was strong, acting the mother hen to her group of wary chicks.

Ioan pulled himself from his perch on the settee.

"You need to sit back down, Rathdrum." Tarleton stood in front of him. "Matilda needs a moment before you go up after her. She needs to comprehend fully what we told her. She needs time."

"I understand, but she sees that she was abandoned by almost everyone who was supposed to love her. If I don't go to her now—what will she think?" Ioan watched as emotion played through the older man's eyes. He knew when Tarleton capitulated.

"Very well. I have hurt her enough over the years by keeping our secret. Whatever you do, don't hurt her," Tarleton commanded.

With a curt nod, Ioan walked out of the room.

It took a mere moment for him to make it up the stairs and into his rooms. He didn't know what he would find. Seeing Matilda curled into a fetal position in the corner by the windows had him pondering what had happened between the parlor and their rooms. He made a note to himself to order a piano forte for the duchess's room, since she wasn't using the room for anything else. He knew, instinctively, that some of the problem was her lack of outlet—there was no way for her to express how she felt.

Ioan fell to the floor and pulled Matilda's form into him, hoping that the bit of comfort he could give her would help her through the worst of her thoughts. He didn't speak, he just laid a comforting hand on her back, gently rubbing the area.

"I knew he was holding something back all these years." Matilda sniffed.

Ioan didn't know what to say to this version of his wife—the wounded, the abandoned child peeking through the walls she had built around her emotions. He continued to rub his hand over her back, prompting her to speak when she was ready.

"All these years and I never knew." Her body quaked with the sobs of a lost girl.

Ioan took that moment and pulled Matilda onto his lap and held her close as she bawled. His little pixie needed to be vulnerable for a moment, and he let her longer than he liked, but with all the pent-up anger and sadness, he didn't dare force her to stop when she wasn't ready. He gently rocked back and forth on the floor. Ioan was taken aback when her breathing evened out and a barely audible snore reached his ears.

"I love you, my little pixie," he whispered in her ear as he cradled her to him.

SILAS HAD BEEN listening to the men talk with his sister. Every thing within him screamed for him to protect her from these traitors. Yet, he couldn't take her without alarming his godforsaken older-by-five-minutes twin brother. He couldn't do that because his plan would be shot to hell in a handbasket. Apparently, operation "apprehend Silas" would commence in the morning. He knew the details; he heard every word. Yet, he was trapped into taking the women when they went out on their shopping outing. He would have to adjust his plan. Edinburgh had many places he could hide them, including the underground city.

He had been to the underground a couple of times—enough to know where the shops and homes were located. There were plenty of place to hides in the South Bridge Vaults. He held back a laugh. He knew the score.

Before long, the music room grew quiet as the people went on with their evening—or morning, he knew not which. Silas couldn't determine what time it was from where he stood in the secret compartment in the music room. Something inside him stirred. He had abandoned his conscience a long time ago. Ever since The Priest got Amelia and him out of the burning house by using an unknown secret passage and tunnel—he owed the man his life and fealty—like a knight of old.

He did his best to raise his sister. Yet, she turned into a pick-pocket and then went into the acquisitions business—and that's how The Priest stuck his claws into her. Damn the man! Silas had told him that Amelia must never be sought for a role in the Shadows—he would not allow it.

Silas' loyalty nearly faltered when he caught wind of her seeking the cypher at Tarleton's house. There was nothing he could do without risking her life. That's when The Priest told him that the true cypher was a person, the new Duchess of Rathdrum.

The duchess was the only person who knew how to decipher the code—that was still alive. The only other person had died under mysterious circumstances seven months earlier. He had heard that it may not have been mysterious at all but poison. He knew one other Shadow agent who use poison—his protégé.

This would all fall on him if things ended badly. Silas needed to think and contact his man in the underground.

ANTHONY KNEW THAT something was going to happen—he didn't

know what, but he knew it would. The tingle on the backside of his neck, the hair on his arms stood straight, and years of honing his instincts told him that something was going to happen—and soon.

He glanced over at Elijah who stood stock still, his eyes surveying the room, looking for anything out of the ordinary.

Anthony knew in that instant they would need to keep a wary eye on Matilda and Amy. In his very soul, he knew that the women were in trouble. Tomorrow would tell the tale.

Into nothing he bellowed, "You better not harm them, you bastard!"

Anthony turned and made his way up to his rooms—the worry remaining that he was being watched—almost thinking that there was something wrong with him.

Anthony opened the door to his rooms; a candle flickered next to the bed. He didn't usually place a candle on the stand on either side of the bed—the bed hangings were too close for comfort. One bad night away from being burned alive in his bed—it wasn't exactly the way he would choose to die.

There was a lump in the middle of the bed, a soft snore, and then the lump moved—Amy. What was she doing in his bed? No, this wasn't happening. No.

"What took you so long?" Amelia asked from the bed.

"I was speaking with Matilda, Rathdrum, and Elijah. What are you doing in my bed?" he asked.

Amelia straightened up in the bed, letting the divot fall about her waist—and his mouth went dry. All the blood in his body traveled south in the barest of moments—his cock springing to life, liking what he saw. This was not happening; at least, not tonight—or anytime soon. He would need a ring on her finger first.

"I want you, Amy, but being the honorable man that I am—I cannot in good conscience make you mine without the blessing of the church and your brothers. Until then, you will sleep in your own bed." He placed his hands on his hips and waited.

Amy reluctantly got up from the bed, pulling the bedding with her, God help him if Elijah saw her like that—or even the servants. He was more than half tempted to keep her until early in the morning, but again, he needed to get the temptation away. He pivoted and opened the door in time to see Elijah slipping into his room.

Damn and blast! It wasn't going to be easy. Especially since Amy padded over to where he was and slipped her arms around him.

"I don't have to leave—" Amelia started.

"No! You cannot. I want to be honorable and certain that we can be together before I allow you to sleep in my bed."

"Anthony, we have so much to make up for. I don't want to waste any more time. I want you and I know you want me." She stroked one hand over the muscles in his arms.

Anthony hissed in pleasure in response, his manhood taking charge, his honor slipping.

"No, not tonight, my angel—but soon. I promise." He lifted her wandering hand and kissed it. He bit his lip as she removed her hands and stepped away.

"Just don't make it too long, Tony. I don't want to miss out on too much time," she said as she side-stepped away from him and into the hall.

Anthony shook his head. He promised himself in that moment that he would do anything to keep them both alive long enough to walk down the aisle, have a couple children, and grow old together.

Chapter Twenty-Four

MATILDA STRETCHED OUT her arms as she yawned herself awake. Ioan's arm lovingly held her to him. She truly needed to get ready for the day. There was a long day of travel and shopping ahead of them—even longer knowing that there may be an abduction somewhere along the way and she couldn't help but wonder if it was preventable.

Matilda knew that they would be at their most vulnerable in the carriage—even with the out riders. There was just too much land to cover and they would be exposed the entire way to James' estate. Her plan seemed woefully ill-prepared—and it scared her.

"Come back to bed," Ioan moaned from where he was lying.

"I've got to prepare for our trip to Edinburgh. I can't stop feeling that something is going to go wrong." Matilda combed her fingers through her hair.

"I think you aren't the only one. Tarleton looked like he had reservations too."

Matilda nodded. She knew that Uncle Anthony was pensive about what was planned for them. Of course, she didn't like the thought of being bait, but she knew that Amelia and she had backup.

"If you continue to worry about it," Ioan started, "you may make mistakes. Relax."

She knew her husband had spoken the truth. She couldn't use logic to explain how she felt, so she locked it away inside her mind. She took a moment longer and then went about her morning ablutions.

An hour later, Matilda strode into the dining room, the other guests already gathered for their morning meal. The tension in the room was palpable—thick and worrisome. Everyone seemed to be on edge, just like she was. Matilda weighed her options. Taking her seat, she filled her plate and began to plan a better option.

SILAS HAD SNUCK out of the ducal manor house late in the night to make it to Edinburgh to secure his own mission. The Vaults housed many shops, but the one that he needed was the illegal distillery. They had a dark corner where he could hide his sister and the duchess until he could interrogate her for the cypher. Something inside him knew it wasn't going to be easy. The duchess was like his sister—she had a lot of mettle. She had wit and an inner shell that was harder than any metal known to man.

Silas couldn't help but feel respect for the woman—and that was something he wasn't prepared for. He couldn't do what he needed to do if—he shut down the thought. *Focus, you damn fool,* he chastised himself.

As he strode through the underground, he couldn't understand the sense of desperation that permeated the atmosphere. It was dingy, smelled of human excrement and the carcasses of the animals that were butchered in the Vault for sale on the streets, and the gazes of the people as he walked by unnerved him.

"Aw, Mr. Black, I wasn't expecting to see you so soon after your last visit." A voice brought him to an abrupt stop.

"Yes, I need the use of your back corner." Silas knew it would cost him.

"For The Priest's work, eh? Fine, but it will cost you. Are you willing to pay the price?"

Silas took a moment to weigh his options. Either he took the bait and tried to take the duchess and his sister on the road, or he took them in the city. He knew the risks either way, but why was he second-guessing himself?

"What is the price this time?" he asked.

"There are some gentlemen—" Silas heard before he stopped listening.

"…that I would like to be dispatched."

Oh, sweet Mary and Joseph! No matter where he went, carnage followed him—sure, he was the best at what he did, but he wanted out, desperately. Just like with the distillery owner, The Priest had a price if he were to retire from his role in the Shadows. The price was his life—he knew too much.

"I will pay it," he agreed.

"Very well." The man nodded and slipped him a crumpled slip of parchment—with four names on it.

Silas eyed the man. He pulled out his pocket watch, which he could barely see in the dimly lit underground. He still had time to get to Rathdrum's estate. He had changed his options. He could go through with the abduction, which would surely land him at Newgate, or he could have a conversation with Tarleton about the Shadows.

He had to decide quickly because it would determine his course of action. His contact in the underground was no longer loyal to him—and that scared him more than it should.

Silas glanced down at the names again. Each of the men on the list were currently at the Rathdrum estate—he made his choice and there was no turning back. He raced out of the Vaults and to the mews to procure a fresh horse for the ride back to the ducal estate. He may be able to catch the carriage at the viscount's estate instead.

Once he got the horse, he climbed onto it and pushed the beast into a gallop. He needed to get to them as soon as possible.

MATILDA HAD WORRIED the entire way from the Ioan's estate to James'. Yet, the hour-long carriage ride was uneventful. She stepped down from the carriage. A woman, much taller than her with red hair, an infectious smile, and green eyes bounded down toward them.

"You are finally here!" The woman beamed. "I am James' sister, Gloria. I have wanted to meet you for long, but my dear brother kept me here."

Matilda had never known the love of a brother, but she could imagine what it would be like by the way Gloria was acting. She could see herself becoming friends with her. Gloria's bubbly nature made it easier for Matilda to feel comfortable—which was a feat all on its own.

"Are we expecting anyone else?" Gloria pointed toward a lone rider approaching them.

Matilda glanced over her shoulder in time to see a man with chestnut hair and a full beard to match jump down from his horse and toward the unsuspecting duo.

"Silas, what are you doing here?" exclaimed Amelia as she alighted from the carriage, James following close behind.

"Don't be naïve, little sister. We both know what I was coming here to do. That has changed. I need to speak with Lord Tarleton, with all due haste."

"We are here," came Uncle Anthony's voice from behind him—and Matilda couldn't help but smile. She had known that Elijah, Ioan, Uncle Anthony, and Finn were just behind the carriage.

"You have a problem."

SILAS DIDN'T MINCE words. "Someone, other than me, is double crossing you. My contact in the Vaults gave me this list." He handed Tarleton the crumpled list of names.

The look on the spy master's face told Silas that he knew what that list meant.

"Instead of doing what you were tasked to do, you came to us—why?"

Silas surveyed the crowd of faces around him; his gaze landed on his sister. "The man who saved us from the fire, he promised me that he would not recruit Amelia. He broke that promise when he hired you to steal the cypher."

"What else, brother?" Amelia spoke through clenched teeth.

"While listening into your conversations, I began to respect the duchess's intellect and creativity. Something in me said that it wasn't right. For the first time in a long time, I couldn't go through with it."

Silas glanced down to the young woman with the red hair and large green eyes. He felt a spark that he had never felt before. He held her eyes with his and knew that he could have a future. He sighed contentedly.

His brother, Elijah, stepped up to him. "This isn't done. My friends still have a price on their heads."

Silas nodded. He knew that someone would take up where he had left off. Then a memory took root in his mind, as if he was living it and that it wasn't in the past.

"Your Grace, have you noticed anything strange about your staff here in Scotland?" he asked, and then continued. "I recognized the butler. He looked much like the man who saved Amelia and me. But, his eyes didn't seem as cold then."

"I did notice that our butler had the same mannerisms as my father. The two could have been like brothers."

In that moment, Silas knew they had found the double agent. The butler had not been in the house when he tried to break in. His contact at the Vaults knew that Silas would apply a secondary plan. Damn and blast.

"I see where your thoughts are going. You didn't realize what you were doing. You were manipulated into believing that we were working for the enemy when, in fact, you were. The Shadows need to be shut down—forever." Elijah tried to ease his trepidation.

"I need to make this right, and I will see it through to the end. I will either witness the man hang or get a one-way ticket to Australia," Silas quipped.

"And you will, but first we have to deal with you," Rathdrum said furiously.

"I will gladly accept any punishment you deem necessary." Silas's mind raced with the possibilities—none of which would be pleasant.

Tarleton smiled. "I was hoping you would say that. I could use your skill set on the Continent for a while until this case comes to its conclusion. You will need to spend a few weeks with me to go over the training you received and what you know about the Shadows."

Without any thought, he agreed. First, they needed to find the butler, question the man, and send him to whichever kind of hell Tarleton decided to send him to.

He stole a glance at the beautiful redhead. He would take his chances—for her, if her brother would allow it. They had just met, and yet, he knew that she would be his. He longed to get her name and to get to know her, but that would have to wait.

Silas and the men climbed back onto their horses and took off towards the Rathdrum estate.

Chapter Twenty-Five

MATILDA, STILL STANDING next to Gloria, breathed in the dust as the men left on their horses. Well, they had better get started back to the house. From beside her, Gloria knew that her new friends were leaving.

"Can I please go with you?"

Matilda glanced over at James. "She can come with us. Or we can stay here until you catch the man."

She could tell that James was thinking about his response before deciding on the matter. Matilda didn't know whether Gloria had the same training as Amelia and she had; if so, she didn't see the danger.

"Very well, but stay near Matilda at all times and remember what I taught you."

"Thank you, Jamie!" Gloria jumped up and down.

Matilda cocked an eyebrow. "Jamie?"

"It's my nickname for him when I was younger," Gloria responded

"I may just have to remember that." Matilda giggled.

She could hear a *hmph* come from James. She couldn't help herself from laughing. "I promise never to use it unless I'm cross with you."

Slowly, the laughter quieted and she smiled at Gloria's exuberance. She also loved that Gloria had been taught to defend herself just like Uncle Anthony had done for her. She could train with Gloria, that was if Ioan would agree when things finally calmed down around them.

"Well, Gloria, are you going to get in the carriage? The men are well on their way home."

Matilda was not surprised when her new friend joined her and Amelia in the carriage. She hoped that by the time they got back to the estate, the men had already apprehended the culprit.

IOAN COULDN'T BELIEVE the twist of fate that occurred. He had recognized who Jeffers was. How could he have not seen it all these years? *The bastard!* He bellowed inside.

Ioan noticed someone standing in the circular drive—then darted out to the moors. The desolate, scarce spaces were traitorous. Not a single tree was visible for miles. Except for the occasional tuft of tall grass, short shrubs, and boulders—it would be nearly impossible for the older man to escape. Unless he knew a secret that Ioan didn't even know. He knew the moors intimately; he had learned their secrets as a child. He had learned to navigate the bogs that ran throughout the land. He couldn't help but wonder, though, how well Jeffers knew the land.

If Ioan's conclusions were correct about the older man, then he had been at the estate for most of his life—if not all of it.

An idea surfaced; the man had always been part of the staff but never part of the family. Ioan had leverage, possibly. *Maybe— damn,* Ioan said to himself, *there was a different game afoot.* With no children, Ioan's uncle, the bishop, would inherit if Ioan were to die. Now, that wasn't an angle he wanted to consider at all. Especially since the two men had always been close.

"Did anyone else see the man run off into the moors?" Finn said as he rode up to him.

Ioan nodded in agreement.

"If the man did go out into the moors, I will need someone

with me to help track Jeffers down. Unfortunately, there are bogs and are extremely hazardous—"

Ioan cringed when he said it, but he knew that the bogs could be deadly. There had been a mishap when he was younger. One of his elder brother's friends had not known of the bogs and got lost—and nearly drowned. Ioan had been nine years old at the time—and it had scared the hell out of him.

"You father taught me how to get through the maze—that's what he called it," Tarleton said as his horse came to a stop beside Ioan's.

"I think I will wait for the carriage. Though, I lived here most of our holidays, I don't feel comfortable enough to make it through the maze. I will send James out when he comes back with the girls," Finn commented from behind.

Ioan knew that his friend was more than competent enough to find his way through the bogs. He knew that Finn's fear was of the water—of drowning, due to an incident when the man was a boy—and still, he had never learned to swim.

"Plus, Andrew needs help with the three ladies—unless Gloria comes with, god forbid." Finn laughed.

Ioan knew that Finn spoke the truth. Damn. Matilda would run into the moors to avenge his family's deaths—all the while side-stepping the bogs. Though the image in his mind was humorous, he knew that the visualization was nothing compared to the reality.

"I can imagine it now. I would rather have you there also. My little pixie can get into a lot of trouble. Remind me, when this over, to tell you how I came to be married to her." Ioan chuckled.

"Don't remind me, Rathdrum. I am still upset that Percy left me out of the whole thing."

"We won't let you miss out on anything—such as—"

"You better not say 'christenings,'" Tarleton exclaimed.

"Not yet, my lord." Ioan smirked. He couldn't help but rile Matilda's uncle.

Tarleton threw his head back and guffawed. "It will be a

matter of time—which we are running out of if we don't catch up to that bastard in a hurry."

MATILDA RELAXED WHEN she saw the façade of the manor house. She almost expected someone to jump out into the carriage's path—highwaymen or some such rubbish. From what she had heard, there hadn't been any highwaymen in years. Did Scotland even have highwaymen anymore? She couldn't help that her mind wouldn't stay quiet. So many questions—so few answers.

As the carriage came to a stop, footmen rushed to open the door to help her and the others alight from the carriage. Matilda surveyed the area around her. She could feel something was wrong, yet nothing seemed to be different than when they left. She glanced over her shoulder and dismissed the tingling along her spine.

"Don't worry, Maddy, I feel it too," Amelia said as she strode up to her, followed shortly by Gloria and James.

Matilda waited. "I don't see any movement inside the house. Shouldn't the servants be up and about?"

James nodded as he raised his finger to his lips in a gesture to tell her to be quiet.

"What's happening inside the house?" James asked the footman.

"Lord and Lady Rosemont are tied to chairs. They were beaten horribly," the footman replied.

Tears threatened to spill from Matilda's eyes. Her friends were in trouble. God, she hoped they were alive. She couldn't live with herself if something happened to Beth and Andrew. Her friends had decided to spend most of the time by themselves, only coming out of their apartments when Matilda performed for the guests. It was under her watch that they were held against their own will. They were supposed to be safe in her home. Anger took the place and she felt herself turn into an avenging angel rather than Ioan's pixie.

"Who did it?" Matilda was determined to make whoever did it pay. No one would ever hurt her friends and get away with it and live to tell the tale.

Then, in the distance, a lone rider became visible, entering the circular drive. She recognized the man instantly—Finn. As he rode closer, he jumped from the horse and coaxed the animal to run alongside him.

"Ioan needs you in the moors as soon as you can. I will stay with the ladies." Finn deposited the reins into James' hands and huddled the women together.

Matilda watched as James pulled himself onto the horse and hurried into the distance. What had she landed herself into? She had been part of this for years and still didn't understand what this was about.

"Well, ladies, shall we go inside?" Finn asked.

"…but, my lord!" the footman exclaimed as he crossed paths with Finn.

"What is it?" Finn glared at the footman.

"There is a problem in the house—"

"For God's sake! Stay with the ladies and I will go in and clear the way," Finn said as he stormed up the stairs and into the house.

Matilda watched on as everything unfolded around her. It had never occurred to her that things weren't as they seemed—that was, until Finn disappeared into the house. The footman glared daggers at her. She smiled to herself. It was apparent that the man had no clue with whom he was dealing with.

"You are mine," the man sneered at her.

Matilda shook her head and chuckled. "I don't think so. Who are you are what do you want with us?"

"You really don't know?"

"It must be something to do with murder and mayhem, but I don't know much about anything," she replied. She didn't want to give away too much. She would much rather the "footman" believe that she was too naïve as to what was going on than believe that she knew too much.

"I don't believe you. The Priest wants you alive, but I would like nothing more than to end your life right now."

It dawned on Matilda that the man was a Shadow. Could he have been responsible for the deaths of Ioan's family?

She cocked an eyebrow. "I don't think so. There is one thing you have failed to do; you failed to do research on those who you are detaining. You underestimate us."

She nodded her head in a wordless command to the other ladies, who took a couple steps to either side of her—flanking her. She pulled knives out of her skirts, Amelia pulled a knife and one of the old dueling swords from her skirts, and Gloria pulled out a gun from hers.

"I would advise that you not move, whoever you are. When we get into the house, I want you to write a letter to The Priest before our men get back. If you don't do as I ask, I will treat you the way you would have treated us. Am I clear?" Matilda waited for the man to acknowledge her words.

The man acquiesced and put his hands in the air. "You will pay for this, Your Grace. You will pay for this."

"I sincerely doubt it, but if it does come to pass, I will come across your master rather than yourself. When that day comes, I will gladly stand toe-to-toe with him on a field of honor and—I will win. Make no mistake about that. You have put my friends and my husband in danger. You will rue the day that you came to this house." She pulled a strip of cloth from her hem and tied the man's hands together. Once Matilda checked that the knot was secure, she pushed the man toward the house, a smug grin on her face.

✦

Chapter Twenty-Six

IOAN DIDN'T KNOW how, but the man had disappeared. His men had scoured the moors for hours—nothing. He couldn't imagine where Jeffers was, and there was nowhere else for him to look. They had searched behind every boulder, every bush, and anything standing above five feet tall—nothing.

Ioan glanced up at the sky and noticed the sun dipping below the horizon. "Well, it looks like we need to get back to the house before we lose the light."

"Ha! You just want to see that beautiful woman you call wife," James said as he whipped his horse around and trotted back toward the house.

"Yes. Yes, I do." Ioan couldn't disagree with his friend. He missed Matilda. He worried about her, though he didn't need to since she was safe with Andrew and Finn.

"Let's get back then. There is no sense in keeping up tonight. The man is now gone," Tarleton agreed.

Tarleton and Ioan followed James as they rode back to the house in companionable silence, not knowing what to say to his wife's uncle, if there was anything to say to him. The ride back gave Ioan time to think about his venture—something that he hadn't done since this whole mess came to light. He needed more men, men that he trusted, and that his men trusted.

Ioan found himself in the hall a short time later wondering if he had landed himself in some fictional land. His pixie stood in front of a chair that someone had pulled into the hall and was pointing a knife at the person sitting on said chair. It would have been comical if it hadn't been Matilda thrusting that knife at a man in—livery? What in the?

"What is going on?" Ioan bellowed.

"Oh, there you are! Just in time. This man is an imposter, sent by the Shadows. He beat Andrew and Beth. The doctor is with them right now, Ioan."

His anger was holding on by a thread. "Do you know where Jeffers is?" Ioan asked the imposter.

"He disappeared when I heard galloping horses approaching. I don't know where he is." the imposter said through closed teeth.

"Oh, love, here's a letter for The Priest. This man said that they leave messages at a certain location in London. It looks like we might want to take another trip to London soon." Matilda smiled.

Ioan chuckled. The imposter must have underestimated his lovely wife. "Well done, Pixie. I'm proud of you. I will have one of my people get the magistrate from town to detain this gentleman. We still have one person to find—Jeffers—and he is all mine."

JEFFERS, HAD SPENT his whole life in servitude to the Duke of Rathdrum—the old and then the new. He knew that Ioan knew his secret months ago. He looked more and more like Ioan's father, which was both a blessing and a curse. The only difference was Jeffers had his mother's blue eyes. There wasn't anything good to say about his mother. She was a whore—a goddamned whore. A well-paid one before she came to be with child.

He was the same age as Ioan's father, and it had been a sacrifice for his father to have him in the house. He was raised alongside his half-brothers, he had the same tutors, and the same education. Yet, he was illegitimate and would never hold the title. When his father died, his brother became the new duke—and Jeffers coveted what he couldn't have. That was, until he met The Priest. He knew who the man was—in fact, he knew the man very well indeed.

He had grown to know every nook and cranny of the estate. He had made sure that he knew everything and everyone on the grounds. He was a vital part of the house; it would not function without him—the duke wouldn't function without him. Jeffers smiled to himself.

He had to give it to his nephew's wife. She was a spitfire, underestimated at every turn. He shouldn't have been shocked when he witnessed Ioan's little pixie push Mark—the imposter posing as a footman— through the front door and into the hall. The woman would be a delight to kill, but his time was running out. It would only be a matter of time before they found his hiding spot behind the picture of Ioan's mother.

Why wait? Why elongate the inevitable? So, Bryan Jeffers, the former butler of Rathdrum Hall, opened the false door to where he was hiding and strutted down the stairs. His nephew wouldn't kill him. Oh no! His nephew, Jeffers knew, would send him in a one-way ticket to Australia. Little did the man know—Jeffers had a contingency plan—which was already put into motion.

Jeffers moved into the hall where the Valor and Honor men were interrogating the imposter. A look of surprise crossed the imposter's face as he strode further into the hall. Jeffers pulled the pistol from his coat, aimed, and shot the man. He didn't mind where; the imposter was a thread that he needed to cut before everything went to hell.

"What in the?" Ioan watched as the imposter collapsed and died with a strangled sound coming from his mouth.

"Oh, you mean the dead man? I couldn't leave him alive. He knows too much, Ioan. He is expendable."

Jeffers knew the questions were just about to start, but he

would answer them before his nephew asked.

"So, you've figured out who I am. I don't need to explain that I am your father's illegitimate brother. You've already found that out, thanks to my dead friend." He tilted his head toward the imposter. "What you don't know is that I have been planted here for years—waiting for the opportunity to arise to finally do away with the Dukes of Rathdrum. Unfortunately, that time isn't now. It looks like I might have a bit of traveling in my future. Am I right?"

His nephew was speechless. Well, Jeffers had no plans on telling anything else. He would not share his secrets with those upholding the law and the secrets of the Crown. "Well, are you going to get me aboard that ship in Edinburgh waiting to transport me to Australia? You didn't know I knew about that, did you? Let's get this over with." He held his hands in front of him, waiting for the shackles to be put on.

This would not be the end of the things. Ioan must know that. The new duke would never be safe if Jeffers was still alive, even from the other side of the known world. Maybe, one day, Jeffers would have his revenge.

IOAN HAD NOT been prepared to have Jeffers to just walk into the hall and surrender himself. He had not been prepared for the man to know about the ship ready to depart Edinburgh as soon as Ioan could get there. He had not been prepared for many things. He shook his head and proceeded to shackle Jeffers and walk him to the carriage that was still waiting in the circular drive from earlier, the horses still hooked up. He would have to speak with his darling wife and household staff when he returned from town.

Many hours later, Ioan strode back into Rathdrum Hall. He had seen his uncle onto the ship and locked into the cabin that would hold him until he reached his destination. He knew the man was intelligent and somehow knew that Jeffers would find a way to escape, but not on his watch—or that of James' captain.

Ioan heard laughter and music drawing him toward the music room. Matilda sat at the piano; the others were dancing between the chairs and lounges scattered around the room. He strode to where Matilda sat and thanked God that they had all made it. There were two things left to do. They may have survived this battle, but they still hadn't found the killer, or who The Priest was.

Once the Valor and Honor men ended this, they would go on to help the rest of the *Ton* with their mysteries. Ioan didn't know where his venture would take him, but he knew that the men at his side—dancing, actually—would be there for as long as he needed them. Ioan knew they had a long journey ahead, wrought full of danger—and it would be worth every moment. He was okay with that.

He listened to the music Matilda was playing, and when her hands came to rest on the piano forte, he pulled her into his arms and kissed her.

"My darling pixie, I love you," he whispered into her ear, just for her alone.

She smiled up at him and whispered back, "I know, and I love you too."

Epilogue

J EFFERS HAD BEEN waiting months for the bloody ship he was on to go around the horn of Africa, where his contingency plan was waiting. In a previous lifetime, he had known a dubious captain of a ship of miscreants—pirates—who owed him a rather large debt. When he realized that he had one option open to him at Rathdrum Hall, he called in the debt. Isaiah Mayhew, the captain of the *Fury,* couldn't say no.

The boom of canons broke the silence. Jeffers had worked tirelessly trying to break out of the shackles that he had been placed in—and just earlier that morning, he had finally gotten himself free. Another boom sounded, and another. Shouting on deck had him smiling. All he had to do was to get up on deck, dive into the water, and swim toward the *Fury.*

Luckily, for him, one of the cannon balls snapped the rigging on his bed and created a giant hole in the hull of the ship. *Thank God for small miracles*, he said to himself. He dove into the sea in time to see the main mast splinter, and the ship was rendered useless. Jeffers smiled yet again as he swam toward the waiting ship.

Once Jeffers climbed onboard the *Fury,* Mayhew was waiting for him.

"You do realize that not just your family will be after me, but the Crown will be too," Mayhew stated.

"I do, but you didn't worry about it when you agreed to this.

I need to lay low for a while and then I will end my nephew and his friends. I think I will start with one of his friends."

Jeffers knew that Mayhew was waiting for the other shoe to drop. The American man was not the brightest pirate captain—well, he was really a privateer—Jeffers had ever met. The man was too soft. Too everything. A debt was a debt, though, and the man's debt was now clear.

"I think I will start with James Kirby, Viscount of Riverton," Jeffers said as he glared at the other man. "And I will make sure that my nephew is there to see it!"

The End!

About the Author

I am a single mother from Minnesota to a little boy. When I'm not working or playing with the "Little Pirate Lord", I'm writing my next book. I have books in two different series, right now. Ironically, the characters in my Wellesley/O'Brien Saga are the descendants of the characters in my Rakes and the Crown Series. I am also playing with a mystery series that may be part of the same family.

Social media links:
Facebook Author Page: facebook.com/JessicaAClementsNavarro
Facebook Reader Group:
facebook.com/groups/2497384330578831
BookBub: bookbub.com/profile/jessica-a-clements
Goodreads:
goodreads.com/author/show/18576993.Jessica_A_Clements
Twitter: twitter.com/JClementsauthor
Instagram: instagram.com/jessicaanneclementsauthor
Website/newsletter: www.jessicaanneclements.com
Amazon: amazon.com/~/e/B01LZNFGST